KRAA

The story of a crow

KAKIYAN

The story of a crow

Capt.
Elmo Jayawardena

© Elmo Jayawardena

Second edition 2019

ISBN 978 - 955 - 21 - 2795 - 3

Cover design
Udara Chinthaka Andrado

Sri Lankan edition printed by
M.D. Gunasena and Company Printers (Private) Limited.
20, St. Sebastian Hill, Colombo 12. R - P - 2007 - 05/2018

Perhaps a crow knows more
than you and me!

To Dil
(The prototype Mama Alice)
With gratitude and love

"Daring, and original. Jayawardena gives us an aerial view of the human condition."

Professor Yasmine Gooneratne
Colombo

"Kakiyan is a must read for all thinking people. It inspires us to reflect upon and improve the way we treat each other and all living beings that we share the world with."

Diva Sandrasagra
New York

"A fascinating biography of a crow and its view of our lives as humans. A fable of how important it is to learn sound values and live by them."

Dr Maria Wessman
Stockholm

"Imaginative and delightful insights from the world of crows, with heroes, villains and human alter egos. A leisurely but thought provoking read that upholds acceptance and commitment to life."

Professor Shehan Williams
Colombo

"Jayawardena continues his penchant for writing, in his latest publication, *Kakiyan*. He uses the metaphor of a Crow to highlight the daily lives of friends. Only 'Kakiyan' can do this in his inimitable style!"

Victor Melder
Melbourne

AUTHOR'S NOTE

Crows are birds that are rarely appreciated. No one really notices a black crow unless in annoyance.

We see them often and curse them often, but seldom do we sing their praises or voice a word of admiration. That's the lot of a crow in our known world.

Kakiyan came to my mind some years ago, and I thought I must write his story, the story of a crow.

I never read any written word about crows, I do not even know whether there are books about crows. I am sure there must be. What I did was, I watched crows - how they flew, how they walked and how they bathed in mud-puddles, and so many other crow-related activities that are common sights in our day to day life.

That is what went into this book, the story of Kakiyan.

I must admit that I enjoyed writing this book more than anything I have written before. The story is all about crows and even if I wrote utter nonsense, they wouldn't know. That saves me from any criticism.

If the book is acceptable as a worthy account of the crow world, I would still be ignored by all crows as to them it does not mean a damn.

So, I had a free hand to write, be creative as much as I wanted and place before the 'Great Ones' a crow-narrated story. As for the 'Great Ones', take a guess, who are they? Read the book and find the answer.

I sincerely hope I can reach you with Kakiyan.

Blue Skies

Elmo Jayawardena
Moratuwa, Sri Lanka.
elmojay1@gmail.com

FOREWORD

Kakiyan: The Story of a Crow is a delightful fable, and despite it being a short story (though Kakiyan is clear it is his 'book') the characters come vividly to life. A teeming crow community living in and flying around the Jacaranda Condominium. Among them, Old Roy, the Grand Master Flyer with memories of faraway places and of the long lost splendour of our beautiful world; Victor of the train journeys, rolling on, breathing in the sweetness of fresh air, hearing only the wind and the chirping of birds; the comic touch of Mooshu and Rami romancing at a football match; the unwavering Black Berry Ro, who insists he just cannot change his lifestyle, but eventually does; Right Turn Eddie, improbably both mischievous and proper; and Cameron, the deep thinker, and how idiotic can a crow get? And of course Kakiyan's immediate family of 'Wise' Alice, Lucille and Rodney. And father, Stanley: family, yet not family.

Some of the earliest stories we know were written as fables, among them the *Panchatantra* and the *Jatakas*. Both were a forest of didactic tales, the *Panchatantra* tales entirely of animals, the *Jatakas* often so, with a moral pathway emerging at the end of each tale. About 300 years back, Bernard Mandeville extended this genre politically in *The Fable of the Bees*, and was much reviled for drawing upon the story of a community of bees, thriving until the bees are made honest and virtuous, the community disintegrating as a consequence. George Orwell's mid-twentieth century classic, *Animal Farm*, was similarly a searing political satire of animals rebelling against humans only to find that their new elite resembles the old. But fables can also be textured around intimate human emotions, within the family, among friends, between lovers, and against baser human instincts. You sense all these raw emotions in Rudyard Kipling's *The Jungle Book*.

Elmo Jayawardena's fable blends characterisation with philosophical musing. It infuses the subtlest of human emotions into the lives of the crow family. The crows are therefore the nicest of the humans. And of course the humans are the most wretched of the humans. In our anthropomorphic view of the living world we can but relate to animals through the lens of human emotions, and it is deeply disappointing that humans do not rate well when viewed though the same lens.

In our modern age fables are then a counterpoint to how science imagines the animal kingdom. Evolutionary biologists tell us that the function of life is solely to pass on our gene pools to our descendants, and that there is no further morality. Where a species does this successfully it adapts well to its habitat and survives, otherwise it goes extinct. But in this evolutionary design we need to distinguish function from purpose, for we humans do have an ethical sense which provides purpose, and need to buttress our reason for existence beyond the bleak logic of Darwinian evolution. While the function of life may be to assist the evolutionary clock, the purpose of life during our brief appearance on this earth must be anchored to reason, emotion and morality. And when these falter in humans, we can tell stories about how much nicer these sensibilities are in animals.

Elmo's fable nests within this space. It is as much a story for children as for adults. A fable to savour, and to delight in the feathered world of the Jacaranda Condominium.

Jayendra Nayak
Former Chairman of Union Bank.

CONTENTS

01. The Beginning   1

02. Fledglings   13

03. Shades from the Past   27

04. Roy Crow, The Flight Expert   39

05. The Train Crow   51

06. Football Matches and Romances   63

07. Some things were sad   73

08. Croco Martin   81

09. Gabriel Crow - The 'Yako Kako'   91

10. Kako Sport   105

11. The Thinking Kako   113

12. A Bit of This and That   125

13. What they did to Croco Martin   137

14. New Nests and Such   145

15. There Never was a 'Forever'   155

01

The Beginning

"Who's going to read the story of a crow?"

That was a common comment on everyone's beaks when I first mentioned to my friends and folks at home that I am going to write a book about my life. Some voiced it aloud, a kind of protest cum ridicule; some muttered and whispered condemnation, and a few others swallowed their opinion in sympathy and made faces appropriate to this literary nonsense by a crow. That was all frontal, the behind the back 'admiration' I could not know, but I am as sure as the rising of the morning sun that there would have been plenty of voiced or mimed mockery at my expense by some kakos who were waiting impatiently to laugh at me.

Oh, well! That is to be expected. Even in the crow world, it is always the norms that are respected. No one wants to believe in things that haven't been done before. And first timers seldom hear the cheers. I knew I would be no exception. But I was determined to enter the book world and place on record what things we did as kakos, so that the inhabitants of this planet would know more about us, our lives, and what a wonderful clan the kakos were. Of course there were a few, very few, who supported me and cheered me on to write our story in spite of the fact that the majority thought I was stark raving mad.

Now the matter is settled once and for all. As in most things in my life, they were wrong and I was right. I wrote the book and you and others who are strangers to me are reading it. That's the proof of the pudding, only this time it is not in the eating, but in the reading.

The story I am going to tell you may not be much of a story, but it is my story, the Kakiyan version of a life well lived. The things that happened to me are all here - the life I led, the dreams I dreamed, the thoughts that filled my mind and the wishes that went sour - they are all narrated here. Some nice things, some wonderful things and of course, a few shameful things too, though they were few and far between. All these add up to hundreds of events, conversations, thoughts and observations which, when strung together, are like a string of multi-coloured beads that represent my crow life in glorious technicolour. It's a long story, and I am going to tell you everything I can remember, from the time I was born to the day I am reciting this tale, but I'll give you the events in simple detail. Of course I may not recall everything that took place or remember them accurately, and might have to fill some gaps in the story with a bit of kako imagination. But the gist will all be there, truthful as far as my memory stretches, with perhaps a little added fantasy to fill in the blanks.

It's important for you to know that what's printed in these pages are not the experiences of an ordinary black 'kak kak" crow; not by any reasonable measure. This is the story of a *smart* crow. I might even add: of a *super* smart crow. The mere fact that mine is the first crow story ever to be published should tell you that I am quite different from the run-of-the-mill Blako Kakos you see in everyday life.

'Blako Kakos': that's what we crows jokingly called ourselves; the words rhyme nicely too, Blako Kakos. But I am a rather different Blako Kako. Though I am blowing my own trumpet now, you'll find soon enough that my trumpet notes are mostly true, that I am in truth, a rather smart crow. Let the story unfold, and you will know what I am talking about. I don't need to 'prove' anything or talk big at the beginning. When the story is finished I'll let you be the judge and the jury, or is it the jury and the judge? We kakos do get confused at times when we borrow metaphors from the Great Ones and try to say things in the way they do.

Now, a word of caution. Don't go mixing me up with that Jonathan fellow. His book was written a long time ago and it's very ordinary. My story has nothing to do with the ordinary. Jonathan was only a small, insignificant gull bird who flew over the sea doing funny things and became a big-shot book-bird simply because he had that long name; and maybe because there weren't many bird stories around in his time. I want to get this point clear before I go any further with this story. Jonathan Livingston and I have nothing in common. He was Jonathan the gull and I am Kakiyan the crow. This is *my* story, Kakiyan's and Kakiyan's alone, and no fast-flying gull story could ever reach the heights towards which I am headed or come anywhere near the vicinity of the things I am going to tell you.

Let me start, but first I must find where to start.

It was my mother who named me Kakiyan.

"I don't want you to be just a 'Kak-ka', I want you to be someone special. For that you need a catchy international name," Mama Alice explained to me.

"These stories about 'what's in a name?' and roses smelling the same whatever they are called are sheer nonsense," she went on. She told me about someone who lived long ago in a faraway land and was known as Bill the Bard. Everybody is expected to know him and have read all these supposedly wise things he's written. I think he was a champion favourite of the Great Ones, to the extent that even we kakos have heard of him.

"Who wants all that William Wisdom about this rose business?" Mama Alice hollered. "Any other name and how roses smell are not for my son. You need a distinct name for the world to know who you are, a name that is pleasant sounding too for people to remember you by. You will be Kakiyan."

The real reason behind all this was Alice Crow's love for foreign things and she modified my name from 'Kakka' as we were commonly called and made it 'Kakiyan'. I guess Kakiyan has an international ring to it, like Robert or Liza or Simon. So I became Kakiyan, the son of Alice Crow, fathered by Stanley Crow, brother to Rodney Crow and Lucille Crow. We were all given foreign sounding names. Lucille, Rodney and Kakiyan.

Most things that happened in our fledgling days including the naming of the children, were controlled by Wise Alice and in some way connected to her. That's what crows in our kako neighbourhood called my mother – 'Wise Alice". She certainly was a very wise and level headed crow, so that many came to seek her opinions and advice, especially when they had couple problems. As for my father, Stanley, he was a bit of a lazy fellow, more like a 'pretend' father who came by once in a way with some food ('for the family' he'd say), but which was usually just some scraps he could not finish eating himself. I guess Old Stan was one of those 'pack home the left-overs' types. The feasts he brought us were nothing more than an edge of a papaw slice or the lousy head of a rotten fish.

That was his great contribution to the family larder. Old Stan wasn't really a bad sort, only big talk, big dreams and not much else; he was just one of those crows who didn't amount to much.

That was Stanley, Stanley of the great stories about what he'd done when he was young. Stan certainly was a great story teller. It took us a long time to realise he was a bit of a brag-master and the tales he told us were mostly borrowed from other crow stories that he conveniently converted and re-told as his own. Stanley's narratives were fascinating, to say the least; full of crow courage and crow cleverness. They were all about how he got the better of the Great Ones. As little crow kids we loved to listen to his escapades and he was good at the delivery, mimicking, acting, and changing voices as he reeled off his dauntless deeds to little kakos who listened in awe with eyes wide-open. Perhaps for believability, Stanley always gave the hero's role in the story to one of his friends and chose to play second fiddle, reserving enough varnish to amply showcase his generosity and heroism.

"Those great people never knew what hit them when Percy and I were around," Stan would boast.

Percy Crow was his good friend and one-time flying mate.

"I would stand guard while Percy darted through the kitchen window, went straight to the table, picked the best and flew back."

He always paused at this point so that we could ask what his friend Percy Crow stole. That too was part of his story-telling, a little break to increase our anticipation. Then he'd continue.

"So what did you steal?" that silly Lucille would always ask.

"Oh, the best cheese money could buy, of course! Those balls of cheese with red covers, and golden yellow insides. Man! How nice they tasted, they almost melted in your mouth."

Lucille was Stan's constant wide-eyed fan and believed everything he said. Rodney and I did the same at first, but little by little the awe faded and the admiration lessened, as Stanley kept repeating stories, often forgetting what he'd said earlier and mixing up acts, events and the crows who had been his heroic partners. Sometimes, while listening to Stanley, we'd steal a glance at Mama Alice. Her manner of shifting her eyes and twisting her head told us that there was more falsehood than truth in the drama of Stan's cheese-stealing fairy tales. Once, when Mama Alice was annoyed with Stanley for some reason or another, she spilled the whole bag of beans.

"That Percy was nothing but a champion coward, more cowardly even than normal cowards. What cheese?" She lifted her head and adopted her regular 'know all' pose. "They never stole any red-covered cheese by charging through kitchen windows as though they were the Light Brigade," she declared, connecting Stan's story to another tale of the Great Ones that was a favourite among the kako elders.

"The best they ever got were some stale crusts of bread edges they managed to scavenge from kitchen dustbins thrown in poor people's back yards, just common crow stuff," she added and scornfully concluded: "Cheese, my foot."

Of course Mama Alice only said these things when Stanley was around, never in his absence. They were always said partly in jest, pure badinage to pass the time, and usually with the truth smothered, but clearly visible to anyone listening with intent. Alice never pretended that her husband was a hero who flew out into the wide blue yonder in shining black armour in search of adventure. To her, Stan was just Stan, the father of her children and the builder of her nest. To Mama Alice he was certainly not the heroic Stanley who stood guard whilst his great friend Percy stole cheese from the Great Ones. He was just her husband, for better or for worse, or for that matter for many reasons, and in all seasons.

We shared our world with many other occupants. I must explain a bit before I go any further with my Stanley stories. You see, we were the crows, the local kakos. Then there were other kakos that came from different places, but we were all crows. All of us were pure black in colour, and we always flew about stretching our wide black wings 'kak-kakfying' like nobody's business. From tree to tree and wire to wire, from rooftop to ground, from ground to tree top, and so on and so forth. Our world was filled with so many other birds too, who shared the open spaces with us and flew around in gay abandon, chirping and chatting in their own tongues of which we knew hardly anything.

We had other friends too, who walked on the ground. Some were friends and some were very good friends, though there were a few we didn't care much for. We left those alone and they reciprocated, which was fine by both parties.

The ones we liked least were the cats. They seemed to have something against us all the time and were always trying to catch and maul us or murder and eat us as if they had nothing else with which to fill their stomachs. Seldom did they succeed, but the battle lines were clearly drawn. The cat and kako divide was well-defined and hostilities were constantly declared with *'grrr meaows'* and blaring *'kak-kaks'* that thundered across our chosen battlefields to tell the whole world a fight was about to begin. Beyond those cats we had no declared enemies except for an occasional 'crawlee' who had the bright idea of stealing and dining on kako eggs or new born babies. They always came silently, slithering up the branches with heads popping up and tongues darting out greedily. These malicious menaces seldom got anywhere; someone in the condominium would notice the slimy crawlee and all hell would break loose.

The suspected egg thief would be pecked and clawed till it fell down, counting itself lucky if it could wriggle away without being killed. These were our semi-enemies, though not all, just the ones who were over ambitious and more greedy than the rest. We had other friends too, water types - frogs from the ponds, tortoises, turtles and even buffaloes who submerged themselves in the mud and said hello to us in their guttural voices.

The crocodiles were even better friends. They lived mainly in the rivers and they often came out to sun-bathe and laze in the day-time warmth, before going back to the water at evening's end. I have stories about these friends, the crocos, that I'll tell you a little later.

But one thing was sure; there was never a single Great One who befriended a single kako. They simply hated us and we in turn hated them probably more than they hated us. That sentiment was historically accepted and proven without a doubt, by the life and times of every crow that ever lived, constantly recalled and related too, so that future generations of crows would know who their real enemies were.

Such was our world, not perfect, but almost, and it has been that way as long as anyone cared to remember, maybe as long as the mountains have stood reaching for the sky and the rivers have meandered looking for the sea.

No one among us, the occupants of this big beautiful world, changed and became craftier or more vicious with the passing of years. We always remained the same. We hated the cats and they hated us. The snakes crawled up to steal our eggs and we pecked and chased them. The crocos were our friends and we remained good friends. The only people on earth who changed and became more vicious and more devious with time were the Great Ones. Their hates and loves rotated and revivified so often that leaving aside kakos and others, even amongst themselves, it was impossible to keep track of who was friend and who was foe: they were that complicated. I guess they themselves didn't know how badly they appeared to the rest of the world. No wonder the Great Ones were such a sad lot. In a way they were shameless too, the way they pretended and led lives filled with lies and deceit.

Let me elaborate a bit about these 'Great Ones'. They lived beneath our trees and were an extremely confused and confusing lot, totally unpredictable in everything they did. That's why we called them the Great Ones. It's not that they were anywhere near being really great, or had anything close to greatness about them. It was our way of ridiculing them. Mama Alice took a lot of time and trouble to explain this to us clearly and in great detail.

"Remember children! They are *not* great, not by any means. They only *think* they are great." She paused at this point to let her words sink in.

"So we let them think that *we* think they are great!" Kak-kak-kak came her loud laugh.

"They pretend like fools to be clever, and we pretend to be fools but *we* live wisely. To know who we are and to know what we can do and what we cannot do, that's Crow wisdom; and that alone has given us the riches of life, much more than they have." To make things clearer Alice would go into didactic mode. "We must always allow them to think they are the best in this entire world," she would say. "That way we'll always get the better of them!" And she'd add with another kako giggle: "There's nothing like making fools think they are wise, that is one sure way to make them into even bigger fools."

Alice Crow was indeed very wise, and she had a knack for putting matters in the correct perspective, using the simplest words and ways. I have a suspicion she had a special reason for hating those Great Ones. It had something to do with an incident that occurred in her family a long time ago, some tragedy that ruined her clan and was connected in some way to the Great Ones. But there is no doubt that her explanation was spot-on. Tragedy or no tragedy we crows always laughed at the Great Ones and knew for sure there was nothing so very 'great' about them. The 'not so great' Great Ones, that's what we laughingly called them. "The fools who *think* they are wise.'

Doesn't that say it all?

So that's how matters stood when I first stepped into this world. Our home was in a Crow Condominium, a huge jacaranda tree that grew at the edge of a small town owned by the Great Ones. Our nest (or shall I call it our flat?) well, whatever the name was, it was located halfway up the trunk of the tree where the branches were thick above and not too thin below. It was covered with thousands of green leaves. Seasonally, the tree flowered; beautiful little purple blossoms that sprouted from every branch, the entire tree smiling flamboyantly with purple petals. The tree was very big and its branches stretched widely on all sides. The upper branches gave us shade from the sun and kept us cool when the days were hot. They also gave us shelter when it rained and kept us dry.

Our flat was spacious; Stanley and Alice Crow had gone to considerable trouble to make it big and comfortable. All the kako flats in the Crow Condominium were built the same with dry twig bottoms and roofs that were open to the skies. Airy, spacious, just right.

There were about thirty plus crow families living in the Jacaranda Crow Condominium, and a host of single kakos too, both male and female. Altogether, about a hundred tenants occupied our jacaranda tree in those days. It was a pleasant place to live, purple at times and green at other times, changing colours with the seasons to break the monotony. That was our home.

Such was the beginning, my early days as I remember them, and the who's who of our family. Now that I've got that part sorted out, let me take you a little further and bring to you some more interesting things that took place in my life, and tell you how and when and why they happened.

02

Fledglings

It was Mama Alice who started our schooling. Off and on Stanley Crow butted in too and contributed his few cents' worth, but it was Alice Crow who taught us what the world was all about, what part we should play in it, and how we should fulfil our allocated roles in life.

"Remember, children," she would always begin in that solemn manner of hers. "You don't have to be too smart. That's a direct route to a downfall. Just be like other crows, do the usual things, and get on with your life." The whole of this first lesson was about being just a regular crow and doing the day-to-day things kakos do.

"See what happened to that little Lester Crow?" Alice brought out the best current example of the Jacaranda Condominium. "Fell to his death trying to fly before his wings were strong enough to support him."

Little Lester lived a few branches up above our flat, and he was a couple of weeks younger than ourselves. Lester was a curious fellow from birth. He used to stretch his neck out, look down at us and grin like a fool. He tried to say hello to us, even before he could speak. One day little Lester peeped out of their flat to see what was going on below. Then he climbed the wall to get a better view, slipped and fell. No wings to flap, no feathers to flap with. He fell straight to the ground like a stone, head

13

first. He broke his neck. And that was the end of little Lester Crow.

Everyone in the condominium was heartbroken about what had happened, especially Lester's parents and his two sisters. Lester was given the usual crow wake with the whole jacaranda community singing a loud and long 'kak-kak' farewell song. We kids joined in and shouted at the tops of our voices. Lester was one of us after all, and that meant something, even though all we could do was to wail and scream. Our little voices were completely drowned in the kakaphony that was going on around the jacaranda tree.

Lester's was a sad death.

"Curiosity killed the crow!" That's what Mama Alice said about it, and she often told the story of little Lester to put some sense into our heads.

"Stay in the nest till you grow stronger, eat the food we bring you, and wait for your wings to feather. It's only then you should peep out and see what's below you." She made her point very clear. "Otherwise you'll end up like Lester Crow."

That lesson was all about staying indoors till our wings were strong. She called it her Survival Lesson and related it on a daily basis till we knew the whole litany by heart.

The second lesson we received from Mama Alice was a language lesson. We all spoke the kako language from the time we were born - that was almost like a birthright. But kakos have long realized the wisdom of learning a foreign language or two. The most useful language for us was, naturally, the language spoken by the Great Ones who lived in our own localities. We learned the basics from our parents and the rest came easily as we roamed around and listened to the Great Ones talk. We came to understand what was said in their speech and how they expressed their thoughts.

In learning the Great Ones' language, there was a strict 'Golden Rule' that was never to be broken: it was strictly forbidden in the kako world to let the Great Ones know we understood their language. This language was to be learnt and used only to our advantage. The rule was laid down a long, long time ago by some wise kakos. This was cleverly and clearly established for our own protection. It certainly saved us from becoming the Great Ones' slaves.

All the animals and birds and even the fish who were foolish enough to let the Great Ones know they knew their language were enslaved and forced to work for them from morning till night without reward. Dogs became guards, horses pulled carts, elephants lifted logs, and dolphins danced in shows, all because they slipped up somewhere in this language business and let the Great Ones realise they understood the spoken word.

"Look at those parrots!" Mama Alice would say. "They thought they were smart to imitate the Great Ones. They even wanted to show they could talk like them. So what happened? The Great Ones caught them, put them in cages and taught them to say some silly words. Prisoners for life!" Mama Alice always drove the foreign language point hard.

"Trapped in cages, saying stupid things and eating seeds from a tin tray - Well! Is that what you call living? If only those idiotic parrots had stuck to flying the skies eating from farmers' fields and keeping their mouths shut, no one would have jailed them in living room cages and expected them to talk. 'Hello hello, Polly hungry, bye bye, how are you? Good morning, good evening, good night, Polly happy Polly happy!'" Alice was good at mimicking the parrots' 'speech'. "Because of their stupid nonsense the poor things lost their freedom and became slaves for life."

Mama Alice always had very clear examples to support her theories. We heard the parrot story repeated whenever foreign languages were discussed in the nest. That's how we kakos learned to handle the Great Ones' language. It was only to be used in whispers, to teach the young ones, and was never to be spoken loud enough for the Great Ones to hear. We knew the vocabulary fairly well as kako kids, and from constantly listening to their conversations, by adolescence, we were practically fluent. The only drawback was that we couldn't read what they wrote in papers and books. This didn't matter too much, as the Great Ones have always been big talkers. They spoke so loudly we could hear everything they said, and that was good enough for us to know ahead of time what they were planning to do next.

The Great Ones had no clue how wise and clever we were. We kakos have only one common language. On the other hand, the Great Ones had many, but, we kakos didn't waste our time learning all of them. No, sir! We only mastered what was spoken in our area. I know, though, of some kakos who were fluent in additional languages too. They are the really bright birds who could figure out almost anything the Great Ones said. This silent mastering of foreign languages was the cleverest part of kako education. No wonder every crow in the world is always one step ahead of the Great Ones all the time, no matter where they live and whom they have to outsmart.

As for what other creatures spoke: well we didn't trouble ourselves to learn their languages as there were so many of them. Most times we could figure out what they said by the way they said it, from their gestures, and by the tones of their voices. Cows mooing, birds twittering and dogs barking - all had meaning which we managed to understand.

There were other lessons too that Mama Alice taught us. They were mostly to educate us about crow life, crow dangers, crow benefits and above all how to be sensible kakos.

"Remember, children, Great Ones will never be your friends. Stay as far away as possible from them! That's the best and the safest thing to do. You only have to look at what they've done to all the creatures who wanted to be friends with them. See those poor bulls over there? They're labouring from sun-up to sun-set pulling loaded carts or tilling fields till they are too old to walk. Then they get their reward! They are sold to butchers to be killed and eaten."

Mournfully she would add: "Oh, but there are worse things than that. See those innocent chickens? The Great Ones hatch them in machines, and as soon as they're born they crowd them into cages and feed them all they can eat. The stupid chickens think it's a great, great life, free arrival, free housing, free food festivals, great party every day to eat as much as they want." Alice's voice was full of disgust. "If you go to the market, you'll see what becomes of them and how they end up. Murdered by the hundreds and hanging by the flesh of their necks on hooks, stark naked too, without even their feathers to cover their shame. A sad and sorry sight if ever there was one! All waiting to be sold, to be spiced up, roasted and eaten."

We would listen, horrified. But Mama Alica had more to say.

"Isn't that sad? From the time they come out of their shells it's a one-way trip to a Great One's kitchen and then to a table where they are carved up with sharp knives, poked with forks and chewed and swallowed." She rolled her eyes at us and prepared to end the lesson on a crescendo of horror. "Gruesome as it maybe, children, it's not quite so bad as some of the other things Great Ones do to chicken. They *grow* them and *kill* them and *pack* them in big body bags, *freeze* them and send them overseas. Why, it is nothing less than exporting murder! The same fate as their local brethren in the market, to be cooked, cut, poked, chewed and swallowed.

"B-but why do they do that, Mama?"

That was Rodney who broke the silence from our side. He was always one for detail.

"Why?" Alice retorted. "There is never a why, Rodney, for anything the Great Ones do." She shook her head at him. "Kill and eat, kill and waste, kill and send abroad, who knows why?" Mama Alice was right. It sure looked as though the Great Ones didn't need reasons to do these terrible things.

"They even have special shops that sell *only chicken*s!" Mama Alice was about to clinch her argument with a final telling point. "*Fried chicken*! Packed in boxes, if you please! And those shops are everywhere, with that silly looking old man with a moustache, wearing a white suit, grinning and inviting people in as if he was the only one who knew how to roast chicken. So good, they say, that people will even lick their fingers."

And that, basically, was Alice Crow's chicken story. She had other lessons too, all equally gruesome about the cruel things the Great Ones did to everyone else who lived with us. The way she told it, sheep, cattle and pigs were treated exactly like the chickens. Raised, fed and killed to be eaten. Even the frogs who leapt about on the ground were not spared, apparently. As for turkeys, ducks and geese, they were grown in farms – "all friendly and nice!" she said - and fattened with care. And then the poor deluded things were killed and loaded straight into an ice box, where they were frozen and kept till it was time for them to be cooked and eaten. We learned from our very young days how cruel the Great Ones were, simply by the wanton manner they relished the death of others. They didn't seem to respect anybody else's right to live in peace and safety on this planet. Mama Alice made sure we were well-versed in the absurd and cruel ways of the Great Ones.

Most of the things she taught us were about survival and safety. It seemed that almost everything that was dangerous to us was somehow, and in some way, connected to the Great Ones. They certainly appeared to be our eternal enemies; and all crow mothers made sure their little ones were taught in detail how to survive the menace of the Great Ones before they ventured out into the world.

"We crows have survived all the dangers we faced by just being kakos," she explained. "We stick to who we are and what we know, nothing more, nothing less."

That seemed reasonable enough.

"Children! Never pretend to be something you're not!" That too was a lesson often repeated, that we received in our young days. For Alice, there was no greater sin than pretence. 'This pretending business' was her favourite tutorial.

"Has there ever been a kako who was caught and sold in a bird shop?"

Mama Alice lifted her head and fixed us with her beady eye.

"Know why?" "Because we don't talk, we're content to wear the same black coat all day and every day, and we only say kak-kak. It's all a matter of not being a pretender, being who you really are and sticking to your kak-kak talk. Those Great Ones don't want any kak-kak noises in their houses. Remember, children, don't ever be a fake; you are no parrots, you are no doves and you are certainly no swans! Be the proud kakos you are, stick to your kak-kak talk and you'll never go to the Great Ones' prisons."

That wasn't all; she had more on the subject of crow identity.

"The parrots aren't the only fools, see those yellow coloured canaries, they go to jail for whistling. Same with the mynah birds, all champion fools with their champion follies of trying to be who they are not and ending up serving life sentences in the Great Ones' cages. No more flying, no more soaring into blue skies, just repeating a silly Great One's 'hello, how are you' words over and over, and whistling Dixie till they die in their jails."

"So listen to me Kakiyan, Rodney and Lucille! No pretending, no talking the Great Ones' language and no whistling sweet melodies. Just 'kak-kak' all you want, the louder the better, be the black kakos you are and fly far and wide as we have always done and you'll be safe forever."

That's how we learned the best lessons of life. Crow wisdom filtered down through the generations was drilled into us by Wise Alice. Though we hardly understood many of the things she said, we listened like obedient little kako children. It was much later, when we grew up and started flying about on our own that we realised how right Mama Alice was. It was all so evident whenever we went into a market place and saw those poor parrots and canaries in small cages, waiting to be sold. There certainly was no song in them, just the sad look of birds sentenced to serve lifetime prison terms in the houses of the Great Ones just so that they could repeat some words and whistle tunelessly to please their owners.

At times, Mama Alice changed course from her usual lessons and went religious to give us sermons. According to her, we kakos are the chosen people of the Good Lord.

"Yes! No doubt at all about that, we are the chosen ones. He gave us one coat, one beautiful glossy black coat, the same for everyone, so that there would be no 'superior' or 'inferior' crows wearing different colours." That was her conviction, and she repeated it many times ever so often.

"You just don't realise how lucky we are to be the way we are!"

"Here beginneth the Sermon of the Single Coloured Coat" my brother Rodney would mutter to me under his breath during the meaningful pause that followed Mama Alice's assertion. Her intermittent pauses were always there to enable us to digest the essence of her arguments in defence of the black we all wore.

"Nothing fancy, but more than enough to get by, simple black for everyone. No multi-colours like rainy-day rainbows. The Good Lord knew how to protect his chosen creatures. Otherwise we too would be like those psychedelic pheasants and peacocks that are killed for their feathers and end up on fancy hats that ladies wear to 'glamour events'. It's our monochrome black that has always saved us." And with that, Mama Alice finished Chapter One of her sermon for the day.

She drew a deep breath, and launched into Chapter Two.

"Now, take those pastel-tinted cockatoos, they always travel abroad, not on independent flights as self-respecting birds should do, but on free rides arranged by the Great Ones. They become expensive international commodities." Alice laughed heartily at her own metaphor. "'Free rides', indeed! Where to? To get their wings clipped, the shameless hussies! That's where, and to perch on an iron stand with one leg *chained*, a life-time living ornament in some Great One's home. Stupid, isn't it? And all because they're born with colours!"

There were many other birds mentioned in her stories and she rotated them so often I am afraid I have forgotten most of them.

"The most awful fate, I tell you, is the fate of budgerigars, chirping in garden cages to look pretty and add colour. They're low maintenance birds too, not like cockatoos."

This was Chapter Three. Mama Alice was attacking the Great Ones on a new flank.

"Budgies are affectionate birds, they like to kiss and cuddle, so the Great Ones say 'How sweet' and jail them. In jail they chirp, make love, and multiply like nobody's business for their owners to make money by selling the little ones." She patted Lucille as if to assure her that *she* was not for sale.

"Born in captivity, and sold for money, isn't that called slavery?" Wise Alice was now in full flight. "That bearded Abraham fellow and his friends were so full of shit with their cry; 'Abolish slavery!' Yes, but that was only for the Great Ones, what about the rest of us on the planet? Nonsense, no wonder somebody shot him when he was watching some stupid play. He only took care of his own kind," she said angrily. We didn't know the 'Abraham' who had roused her ire. All we knew was that he was named 'Abraham', that he had a beard, got shot, and was full of shit.

All according to Alice.

"Everyone wearing the same colour is a great way to live," she declared with strong conviction, shifting to a new subject.

"Look at those Great Ones, eternally fighting amongst themselves because they are born with different coloured skins. Some white, some yellow, some brown and some black and all shades of each colour too." Colour was a favourite weapon when Alice wanted to run down the Great Ones.

"If they were born one colour as we are, they wouldn't have had all those terrible colour-based conflicts to resolve, and that poor Nelson fellow wouldn't have been jailed in an island for so long." That was Alice's number one colour story. It was about this dark fellow who was jailed in his own country for a very long time just because he was black.

She had other examples too in her repertoire, all on the same theme, about being dark and being thought less of for that reason. She often told us about a lady named Rosa Parks.

"Rosa was a poor kako coloured woman, black as night," said she. "Should have had a proper seat in the bus without having to make a protest. Know where all that ended? Buildings burned, houses burned, people killed …. and people walked for a year without stepping into the buses that denied that Parks woman a seat. That country has never been good for anything black, not even for crows. We hear so many unbelievable stories about them and the way they yell how black is ugly. People there hide behind long white cloaks with holes for eyes and a hole for the mouth, they burn crosses and hang dark people to prove how lily white they are themselves." Alice ended her long sermon here. "What a sad thing to kill people because they are black?"

Alice always knew what went on in the world; she remembered everything she heard from other crows and filtered to us the things we needed to know.

"That's their main problem, children," - she was moving into the conclusion, now - "their colour nonsense! I can tell you not one or two, but thousands, maybe millions of stories about how Great Ones fought wars and battles simply because they were born in different colours."

Well, that's how she proved to us that we were God's chosen. It was a simple matter it seemed, of having the same colour, being born equal, and staying equal.

"That too the Great Ones copied from us anytime they wanted equality. In their schools and factories and even in their armies and navies, they wear the same clothes to look the same. They even extend it to whole countries." Mama Alice's colour stories would often go international.

"There is this big land, very big, full of people with half closed eyes, the ones with half a view of the world …." She would say, speaking of some far away place. "Their leader stole our style and made everyone in his whole country wear one colour." Then she nodded and added with pride. "Not our black, theirs was a dull gray, but same purpose, copied from the kakos to be equal; big country, big man, eyes half-closed, but stole our mono-colour method so everyone could match each other and be alike."

Mama Alice knew her history and geography and came out often with facts, interspersed with religion and imagination, to convince us we were the chosen ones. "That one-colour coat alone has saved us from so much trouble." She repeated her praise of the Almighty, who she believed ran 'the creation business'.

"No competition among *us* about who is better dressed and who looks good. That's sense and wisdom for you!" Alice was one proud crow and she really believed that we crows were special. "Some others too tried to call themselves the chosen ones." She changed gears and went for further proof.

"*What rubbish?*"

Here her objection was very strong and here kak-kak was almost a yell. "They were massacred all over the world for centuries and thought they got their own country at last, they're still getting killed and bombed in their own backyard like nobody's business." She didn't tell us who these unfortunate people were.

24

"They were chosen all right. Chosen for punishment wherever they went!" She added that last bit with a trace of sarcasm.

Well that was what Mama Alice was all about, wise and proper and full of love, doing her best to make us strong in mind and ready for a world that we knew nothing about. The lessons she taught us stood us in good stead as we squawked and pecked our way through the hullabaloo of life, and made us often marvel at what a good mother she was to us.

Best of all, she did all this and never asked for anything in return.

I guess that must be a good definition of the 'perfect mother'.

03

Shades from the Past

The days rolled one by one and they were mostly happy days. That was our life, a happy life with no great plans except to take each day as it comes and make the best of it. That's what Wise Alice always preached.

"Children, you must remember that we live moments at a time. If you are hungry, find something to eat. If you feel lazy, go to a nice quiet corner and take time to relax. If you feel full of life, swing your wings and fly, just for the love of it. Let the wind caress your face, look out at the billowing blue sky and say hello to the world. That's what life is all about, just taking moments and doing what you want to do with them, then stringing them together to make yourself a meaningful life in which each day matters."

There certainly was a lot of sense in what she said. Moment to moment, strung together to make the days go by.

Mama Alice took very good care of us in every possible way. Off and on Stanley too made his miniature contributions: the occasional bits and pieces of food he brought home and the way he killed boredom at times with the 'hero' stories he narrated about himself and his friends.

The Jacaranda Condominium was a great place in which to grow up as a child kako. Everybody was happy there, if you didn't count little Lester Crow's tragedy of falling and breaking his neck, nothing that could be called sad happened in our little world and the days simply went from one to another in the best of Blako Kako fun and harmony.

We all woke as the first sun rays lit the sky; light appeared always from the sun rising side and was indeed a marvelous sight to see; how the darkness lifted and vanished like a thief and pale light filtered in to announce the gift of another day. The world went from midnight black to rain-cloud gray to misty wisps of morning shades that pastel coloured our world. Each awakening was often the same, complete in beauty, no more, no less, an equal measure of perfection dished out by the Good Lord Himself in a manner that only He knew how.

The first kako that woke with the first light started the condominium 'kakaphony' which woke the rest of us, and then we all joined in a song to herald the new day. The day's chores had to be done; an early start helped to move things smoothly throughout the day and made all the difference. It's my theory that the popular story about an early bird always catching worms is nothing more than a stupid fiction made up by the Great Ones. We always woke early, but I can't say I know of a single kako who went in search of a single worm on any given day. It's all nonsense.

The first to fly out of the jacaranda tree were Alice's lot, the mama crows who went looking for food for their babies while the rest of the jacaranda crowd milled about jesting and chatting and discussing their plans for the day. Most talk was about where the breakfast could be found. Some stuck to routine and simplified life by sticking to a marketplace or the backyard of an eating house, where the food was sure to be plentiful.

That of course has a small disadvantage; such places offer mainly 'fixed menus,' and their crow patrons have to eat the same thing nearly every day. More adventurous crows went about loafing, seeing the world and eating what they found. Only the bravest dared to buck the Great Ones and steal from their homes. That was the food scene of a kako day. The rest of the daylight time was spent gathering at kako haunts to talk shop and meet friends from other condominiums. Some simply took a day off. They bathed in the morning and basked in the sun to dry their jet-black coats. We all had something to do and we all did what we wanted to do. How much simpler could life be?

We all returned to the Jacaranda Condominium when the sun went to the other side of the sky and the world started to turn black again.

One thing we crows never did was to mess with the day. We woke when the sun came up and slept when the sun went down. No late nights and day sleeps to upset the time table the Good Lord had given to us. Everyone flew back at sunset and we all had a habit of gathering in twos and threes and chatting noisily wherever we could perch: usually on those long electric wires that stretched between lamp posts in the vicinity of the jacaranda tree. That's when we exchanged the news of the day, daily news of who went where and who met whom, and what they talked about, and what they ate, and whatever happened after that.

It was great talk, instant updates of the day's happenings, which wised everyone up to goings-on in the kako world. As soon as the sun went down and the skies darkened, we stopped chatter and went to sleep. The security crows of the Jacaranda Condominium slept with one eye open or sat silent watching the world in case there was some mischief that threatened the nocturnal peace of the sleeping Jacaranda Kakos.

All in all our lives were near perfect as you can see. We were carefree; loved and protected by our families and our community at large. There was yet an inherent and very real 'fear' that we kakos could never get rid of, that was to do with the Great Ones with whom we shared this universe, sadly. Their selfishly motivated actions threatened the life of every kako making us unpredictably vulnerable in our own homes and in our own space.

This brings to mind a fearful incident that happened when we were fledglings in our warm and cosy home in the jacaranda tree.

That morning too was bright and crispy, if I remember right: sunlight creeping through the jacaranda foliage and a listless wind moving the leaves around in a soft musical melody to be heard only by those who listened attentively. Mama Alice had flown out at first light on a food hunt. Lucille, Rodney and I were playing 'Found a Peanut', and waiting for her return to have our breakfast. Stanley was nowhere to be seen; in fact he had been missing for a few days, and we'd thought he was probably doing his usual thing, loafing with some no-good friends of his.

We heard the first warning shouts of kakos from a nearby condominium, just up the road. They were joined by all the crows in the neighbourhood, shouting at the tops of their voices and warning everyone that the Great Ones were up to their devilry again.

Believe it or not they were cutting branches off the crow trees, hefty men in orange suits with large machines and long ladders, chopping the very branches on which we kakos had built our homes. Crows were flying everywhere, warning and moaning at the same time. The entire sky was full of black dots, all screaming protests that fell on deaf ears. Some crow nests had fallen to the ground; they were from lower branches that had been cut off first, and some little crow babies still in them were crying and pleading for their parents. Most of them were injured and dying in their trampled nests. Some mothers who were present and had witnessed the carnage helplessly surrounded their fallen babies. They screamed pitifully, and even attacked the Great Ones who were cutting the trees, flapping around their faces and heads, at the risk of their own lives. A big machine came along to clear the road. It shoved the fallen boughs, the broken crow nests and the crying crow babies into the gutters in one heap. It was a sad sight indeed, as sad as it could be. The moaning of the little ones could be heard even from the drain, then it gradually softened, faded and went completely silent, the innocent paying for sins they had never committed. Only the mournful lamentations of the mother kakos continued, the loss of an off-spring is an incomparable sadness, and that doesn't lessen simply because we are black-feathered crows.

The three of us were shocked and frozen with fear, and shouted at the tops of our voices for Mama Alice. She was nowhere to be seen and we didn't know what to do. We could see the Great Ones coming along the road towards us, chopping branches and destroying crow homes. We knew it would be our turn before long.

"Come on children, get up! Let's get you all to a higher branch." That was Dincy Crow, Lizzybird's mother (they lived some branches above us.)

"Come on, come on," she kept calling, finally she flew down and landed on our branch to get us to move out.

31

It took a while, but we heeded her. Her presence made all the difference, even though it was in mortal fear we climbed to the top of our nest.

"Hop on kids, hop on to this branch," saying so she flew closer and stood on the branch a tad higher than our nest. Dincy Crow was leaning towards us and yelling for us to hop to that branch. Rodney and I managed, and it was Lucille who was so frightened to move. Dincy jumped on to our nest and almost pushed Lucille up to reach the next branch. Thank God that the jacaranda branches were so closely knitted, it was like a little path to hop and move up a branch at a time. With Dincy Crow shouting encouragement we managed to hop higher and higher. We finally reached her nest which was way up high in the jacaranda tree.

"You will be safe now, children," Dincy assured. It was so very comforting to be with her.

It was heartbreaking to watch the Great Ones set up ladders, climb up, and cut off the branch that held our home. We saw it go tumbling down and break into pieces as it hit the ground. Lucille screamed and Rodney screamed and I screamed too. They just broke up our home, our little home where we had lived happily with so much love.

Our screams lasted long and gradually melted into sighs and crying and a gush of tears. We were comforted by Dincy Crow who had become our foster mother in our time of need.

That day the Great Ones did a great job of making a great many crows homeless. Some little ones fell and died, innocent and helpless. Some, like us, were saved by kind crows like Dincy. The Great Ones didn't care; to them we were just crows - dead crow babies and broken crow homes didn't count at all in their reckoning.

The entire morning was shattered and filled instead with unbearable sorrow. Perhaps it was the saddest day I saw in my entire life; nothing that has happened afterwards ever came anywhere close to that terrifying ordeal. I don't think I could ever forget what the Great Ones did that day, no matter how many seasons pass by and no matter how hard I try.

Some time later Mama Alice returned to the jacaranda tree. She'd been flying for food and when she heard about the calamity, she flew back as fast as she could. By the time she came back we were safely settled in Dincy Crow's nest. Mama was shocked at first, then she grabbed and hugged the three of us before crumbling in a heap beside us. I had never seen Alice cry so much. She cried, and gasped, and cried again. We knew she was inconsolable. She had lost her home.

Soon enough Mama Alice took control of herself and plugged her tears. She flew away with a determined face, leaving us in Dincy Crow's care. We knew she went to assist and console crow mothers who had lost their babies. That was typical of Alice, always rising to the occasion, always willing to lend a hand.

"She wasn't shedding tears for your home, children," Dincy explained in the soft and gentle voice that kakos use when speaking of matters meaningful and solemn. "Alice wasn't crying for what happened. Her tears were more for what she remembers, the sheer absurdity of it all." Dincy Crow's voice sank to a whisper.

"It happened a long time ago, before your mother came to live in the jacaranda tree. She lost her entire family. The Great Ones shot them all. Only Alice escaped. She has always wept in her thoughts, but today she wept for everyone to see."

"They were killing crows!" Dincy spat out the words. "They killed the young, the old, the males and the females and even the little ones," Dincy added in disgust. "All because the Great Ones felt the crows were making their cities ugly. Their concrete pillars and their black tarred roads without crow droppings were more important to them than our lives. The Great Ones had tried many times to get rid of us and failed. This was their 'Final Solution'. That's why they shot every crow in town." There were tears in Dincy Crow's eyes.

"The Great Ones killed them all." That's what Dincy said. Every crow on every tree in that whole area had been shot and they had shot at the nests too, to kill even the baby crows. Alice's whole family was wiped out, first her father, then her mother and then her two little sisters. When the shooting had started no crow had flown away, they had all hovered and cried and had lingered around to protect the little ones. Some had even dived at the killers in an absurd effort to peck and fight them off. That was kako courage at its best, mingled with the undying love they had for their brood.

"One by one they all died." Dincy's voice became somber. "Not one flew away, trying to save themselves. They all stayed back in protest and they died protecting their homes and families. Only Alice escaped."

Little Alice had been out on a branch when all this happened, and she had hidden herself in a tree hollow till the shooting stopped. She had huddled there for days, frightened and hungry, and crying all the time till some other crows from far places had come by, found her and helped her to fly to another home. She was so small and frail that she had to fly from tree to tree and stop very often to rest. The little orphan had found her way to the Jacaranda Condominium, and had been given a home there by Vini Crow, who had adopted her, showered her with love, and had later become her foster mother.

That was how Alice became Granny Vini's daughter, not by way of nest and egg and hatching, but by love designed by destiny.

"It was the most terrible thing that happened to us crows for as long as we can remember," ended Dincy.

I still remember what Dincy said and the way she said it. It didn't dawn on me for some time what she really meant. We were just little kakos, after all, too young to understand the Great Ones' barbarity. But I remembered Dincy Crow's face, I remembered her words. A long time afterwards, I realised what that was all about.

No wonder Mama Alice hated the Great Ones. We had heard everything from Dincy; the story was cruel and unbelievably horrible. It was difficult to understand why 'so-called' civilized ones did such uncivilized things to innocent birds who only flew around and lived their own lives without harming anyone.

We'd never before heard this story of how Alice lost her family, and it was the last time too. Alice never spoke of that tragedy. Whenever we asked, she just ignored our request to hear the story of how she lost her loved ones. I remember asking her a few times: Mama Alice, that great story-teller, never obliged.

At that time we were too young to know how painful it would have been for her to recall and relate something that she was constantly praying to forget. She never went back in time to tell us what happened to her family. We only knew what Dincy Crow told us.

It was no wonder that Mama Alice hated the Great Ones. They seemed to have no limits to their wickedness, killing every living thing that walked, flew or crawled in our world including their own kind. That's something we never could understand. Kill your own kind for no reason, and kill crows to beautify their cities. That's cruelty, macabre and totally meaningless, whichever way you look at it.

I've often wondered how it would be if we all got together and found a way to kill all the Great Ones to make our world pretty! No other living creatures on earth ever disturbed what the good God created and gifted to us to live in happily. Even the most powerful among us all, the elephant, he only plucked leaves from the trees and ate them: that's all he did as long as anyone could remember. The lions, so powerful, so strong, just rested in the grass, and when they killed another living thing, it was only to feed their hunger. They don't harm anyone to collect their skin, or sell their meat to another lion. Take a rhino, a bear, or a giraffe, all of them big and powerful, but did they ever want to change anything? No, they wear the same clothes they have always worn and they don't go around killings pheasants in order to take their feathers and wrap them around themselves to look prettier or more handsome.

It's only those vile Great Ones who want to change everything. It's they and they alone who have mercilessly destroyed what was so beautiful in the beginning. We only hear stories of beauty from the older kakos now, but we can see for ourselves that what remains is deteriorating. It won't take long for the Great Ones to destroy everything that's beautiful on the planet.

Yes! It's an unkind thought perhaps, but the world would certainly be a better place if there was some way we could destroy all the Great Ones and eradicate them from the earth as they've done to some others who lived here. It is their endless greed and their insatiable appetite to outdo others that has demolished the sanctity of co-existence and led to this decline towards destruction. The inheritors of the future will have nothing left, be they bird, beast or the Great Ones themselves. It's as if they have made a covenant to this effect, making sure everything is ruined as much as possible, and as soon as possible. Even a simple kako like me with my little kako mind can understand that, so why can't they?

04

Roy Crow - The Flight Expert

We never ran short of experts at the Jacaranda Condominium. For everything that happened in our lives there was an 'allocated expert' kako ready to advise us. We turned to them whenever we needed opinions or advice. Their expertise was vast, and their dedicated assistance was a real day-to-day luxury for the kakos who lived at the Jacaranda Condominium. There were the food experts for example, who knew where to find the best food. Each crow Gourmet had expert knowledge of all the different kinds of things we liked best to eat. You named it, there was an expert in waiting who could tell you where to find it. 'Anything at anytime' was the catch word among kakos where food was concerned and most of us fitted into that category. We ate everything that could go through our beaks to our stomachs. The system was simple and easy, and we were never hungry. Though there were, of course, some semi-fussy kakos who were more selective than the 'anything at any time' kind. What they ate mattered a lot to them and they ate at regular times, sticking to breakfast, lunch and supper slots as the Great Ones did. They had their own expert guides to tell them where to get what they wanted to eat.

And then there were the daring kakos who belonged to an exclusive elite. They ate only what they stole from the homes of the Great Ones, not from their garbage bins or what was thrown into the back yards, but food that came straight from their kitchens and even at times from their dining tables. These kakos were considered fearless, but most of us thought they were foolish, just showing off and taking risks to fill their stomachs, when there was so much good food lying around in abundance anywhere we lived.

There were some specialist crow Gourmets around too, the meat-eaters who operated around the butcheries and got fat eating beef, pork and lamb and whatever other meats sold by the butchers. Our fruit experts covered the markets and knew when the big multi-wheeled lorries unloaded and when the markets opened, so they could pick up the best vegetables and fruit for a vegetarian feast. As young kakos, we always went to the experts whenever we fancied eating something unusual, to ask where to find such a thing; chicken feet, prawn tails and scraps of sugar coated bread. But most of us, most of the time, were easy nibblers, the 'anything at any time' type, who just flew around and ate everything on offer, with little fuss or ceremony.

Well that was the nourishment side of our lives, looked after by food experts of all kinds who were our walking-talking menu cards.

I must not forget the dedicated experts who handled the Jacaranda security. Any threat to us jacaranda crows was their business. They carefully observed everything the Great Ones did that could pose a problem to any of us. Except for an occasional cat or a crawlie it was always the Great Ones who were a danger to us. Only the most senior and dependable kakos were recruited to this security group. They even had a roster made and kept night vigils so we could sleep in peace knowing we were safe.

There was another team of experts who knew and patrolled the skies. They predicted when the rains would come and the days when the sun would shine. That's how we scheduled our flight programmes and knew what days were good to fly on, and on which days it was wise to huddle together and stay at home. Their predictions and readings of the skies were very accurate at all times; real expert stuff, right on the dot.

The most popular experts among us were the Match Maker Crows who found partners for lonely kakos and the nest-making Architect Crows who helped newlyweds build their jacaranda homes. All this was to do with reproduction, what it took to lay eggs and have babies, the fun things in life. No wonder they were popular and much sought after! The sad ones were the Undertaker Crows. They had solemn faces and melancholy eyes and even on normal days they looked a bit forlorn. They supervised the funeral arrangements when one of us died. They gathered everyone together, flew around the dead kako, and led the rest of us in the mournful, sorrowful kako songs reserved for such occasions. Any kako death was announced loudly so the whole world knew we were mourning a kako who had permanently left the fold.

The stern ones among our experts were the Judge Crows. They decided how those who misbehaved should be punished and they had the power to expel anyone from our jacaranda tree for breaking kako laws. It was no easy task to be appointed a Judge Crow. They were specially elected by the elders of the jacaranda tree. Only the most reliable, and those known to be totally honest, had the honour of being elected to the Judicial Branch to become a Judge Crow of our tree.

Yes, we had first class experts. They decided or advised and we followed. That way we had the best choices in life and the best protection in everything we did. That was kako wisdom for you, well-planned and well-laid-out through the ages we kakos have been around.

Roy Crow was the flying expert, the one who knew how best to fly. We children were sent to Old Roy as soon as the fur on our backs turned to little feathers, and our colour changed from the pale rose of kako kids to the shining black coats of adult crows. That was the suit we proudly wore for the rest of our lives. Black to us was absolutely beautiful. When that coat started spreading, we knew we were transforming into world renowned, omnipresent Blako Kakos.

There were five in our batch who went to Old Roy for our first flying lessons. Rodney, Lucille and me from our nest, Jason Crow and little Lizzy Crow from another branch of the Jacaranda Condominium. She was called Lizzybird by everyone, a pet name given to her by her grandmother. Lizzybird was a bit fussy and not so friendly either, but I suppose, tolerable.

We would have had six in our team if that inquisitive Lester hadn't fallen out of the nest and broken his neck.

We lined up on our branch one bright beautiful morning, and waited for old Roy Crow to come down and tell us what flying was all about.

"You've got to learn well, boy: how to fly, where to fly and how to find your way back home." That was the first thing he said to us, the simple essence of Roy's lessons. "I'll teach you all I know, boy." To Roy Crow everyone was a 'boy', including Lucille and Lizzy and all the others of their gender.

"When I finish with you," he promised, "you'll be able to fly even to the moon!" As he said that, a smile decorated his lined face, a wry smile with a matching glint in his eyes.

As his name reveals, 'old Roy' crow was an elderly bird. He lived alone in the highest branch of the jacaranda tree. In his youth he had been the first one among the jacaranda kakos to attempt long distance flights. Old Roy had gone missing for long periods, and had flown over places the rest of us had never even heard of. Roy had been a bit of an adventurous fellow when he was young, and wanted to see the world. He'd done his roaming mostly alone, but sometimes by tagging along with ducks and geese, following them when they flew past our jacaranda tree on their way to warm places as seasons changed from time to time. In those days some of the jacaranda crows did think Roy was a bit mad, kind of footloose and wild. That's what Alice Crow told us.

"Tried to pretend he was half duck and half goose, but deep within he was always a very lovable and warm hearted kako." Mama Alice was soft-peddling on Roy's behalf. That was old Roy's saving grace, apparently: a great roamer, but with his kako soul intact.

He certainly was the most travelled crow in our condo.

By the time he started teaching our batch, his loafing days were over. He mostly stayed put, perched up on his high branch in the jacaranda tree, watching the world go by. One of Roy's wings was bent. Some little hooligan from among the Great Ones had shot him with a catapult and broken his left wing.

"No big deal, boy!" Roy would play down his injury. "It could have been my head." He sarcastically laughed. He always laughed when someone asked about his broken wing. He was a wise kako who had accepted his wingless devalued life and saw no need to grumble about it.

"Just supposing that stone had hit my head? I would have been gone and they would have re-named me 'No-head Roy,' Kak-kak-kak!" and he laughed still more, nodding his unscathed head and swinging his broken wing.

"It's true I can't fly as I used to, but I am still here and that's what matters," Old Roy explained. "Got to look for the silver linings, boy, I've flown far and seen so much, and I still have all those wonderful memories." He often recalled the past nostalgically, perhaps going back in thought to the places where he had once roamed.

"I sometimes dream of the places I've been and then I'm back there in my mind. Yes, I am soaring above the clouds and breathing fresh air, flying over meadows washed by the rain and warmed by the sun. Flying, flying, flying, flying for the love of flying, flapping my wings to the song of the wind."

"That's enough for a lifetime, boy, enough to last me till I finally go away." That last part he always mumbled, speaking almost in a whisper.

Roy Crow first taught us how to swing our wings, the rhythm of which he called the secret to flying.

"Stand firm-footed, boy! Now stretch your wings as far as you can! Now flap them up and down."

He demonstrated this action, his old talons tightly clutching the branch on which he stood, and swinging his one good wing. He flapped this wing slowly at first, then gradually increased its speed till his feathers became almost a blur. Old Roy moved smoothly and gracefully, even with only one wing. We watched and imitated his action as well as we could, our little wings stretched and swinging, and our tiny talons holding the branch we were perched on.

"Not so fast, boy, just keep the rhythm going, like everything else in life!" Roy squawked as our new feathers bit the air, to keep the tempo, while our feet clawed to stay firm on the branch.

"Now ease your feet, lean forward and let go, booooyyys," Old Roy urged as we flapped and leaned and our feet came off in that fascinating magical first leap to fly a foot or two and land. He watched us like a hawk, the five of us, his new students stepping into a new world. We belonged in that world after we learned to fly, one step today and then to the far horizons another day. It pleased the old crow. You could see the glint in his old eyes and the half grin with which he watched us landing safely on the first branch that we could reach. I simply have no words to explain what it meant to us.

We had learnt to fly.

And so we practised flying, it only needed practice and more practice day after day, under the vigilant eye of the Grand Master Flyer, Roy Crow. 'Stretch and keep the feet firm, flap and stay in rhythm, lean and let go'. That was flying. Roy taught us first to fly from branch to branch on the jacaranda tree, and then we learned to descend and ascend all the branches within the Jacaranda Condominium. Then Roy let us go from tree to tree. As we improved our technique, our skills expanded until we could fly great distances, from anywhere to nowhere, our range as limitless as the blue sky that stretched far and wide above us.

There were many more lessons to be learned about flying once we had mastered the first steps. Along with the lessons came stories, wondrous tales Roy told us of where he had been and what he had seen.

"You wouldn't believe till you see them, boy," he'd say. "The mountains alone have enough beauty to last you a lifetime. They are dressed in green, green trees that make it seem as if each mountain is covered with soft parrot feathers, and they just jut out boastfully into the cloudless blue sky. Imagine it – the blues of the sky and the greens of the mountains, and me flying between earth and sky, with cascading waterfalls flowing into silver streams under my belly."

Old Roy Kako was certainly living a different life now, in a different place.

"Boy, you got to see to believe, just like the good God made them and not a single Great One around to spoil it."

"Then there are the little streams joining the big rivers and they all flow to the sea through valleys where no Great One's footprint has ruined them. No one there has cut down the trees or flattened the land to fill it up with cement. The air there is pure and the winds blow with the fresh smell of flowers and wild tree leaves." He closed his eyes and pondered, "I can still smell them," whispered Old Roy sniffing the air in a nostalgic reminiscence.

"They were all there, the mountains, the skies, the trees and the streams, in perfect harmony, the birds flew and the fish swam. But then, they all vanished..." He swung his head in dejection, disappointment written all over his rugged face, "vanished like the mist in the morning, after the Great Ones came and began the ruin."

Old Roy's stories always went way beyond the day-to-day jacaranda talk and the jacaranda tree. It wasn't just flying he taught, but a whole way of living with our wings, about thinking wide and free, and about making plans to someday see at least some of the places that were still intact, just as the Good Lord had made them. That's what that 'Old Roy Boy' slotted solemnly into our little crow minds.

"Got to see the world, boy, someday somehow, flap your wings and go."

The real flying too was taken very seriously.

"You must learn to hover in one place, nice and easy, like pigeons do, leaning into the wind," Roy explained. "You need to linger and watch. There aren't trees everywhere for you to perch and do a look-see." He used these funny words like 'look-see' that only he knew.

"The trick is to put your beak into the wind, boy, and stay stationary." He stretched his head in imitation, and raised his good wing.

"It's so easy, you just got to learn."

That too we practised and we became pretty good at facing the wind and staying in one place, always with our beaks into the wind, our wings flapping in rhythm with minimum effort made, and taking a good 'look-see' at what was down below.

Old Roy taught us to fly fast and short, and fly slow and long, to keep our wings expanded to the furthest extent and to glide like hawks. We learnt to peel off directions to fly with the wind; that was to get a better push. We mastered climbing straight up and diving at dry leaves on the ground, picking them up on the move, imagining them to be juicy pieces of ripe papaw. There were a lot of lessons about speed and power, gliding and relaxing, ascending and descending and flying to stay in one place. Everything we did was watched and corrected by master craftsman Roy.

"You must learn to hold speed boy, that's a golden rule." He was teaching us to fly in a group. "You fly behind one kako, with another kako behind you," Roy explained how to fly in formation.

"Got to watch the speed, boy, or you'll chisel into the front kako's arse by going too fast."

That was another one like that 'look-see' business, chiseling into the front kako's arse by flying too fast. That was Roy, always wise with words, not copied, but created in his own inimitable manner.

"Team work, boy, that's the smart way to fly," Roy often repeated. "Remember, it's no contest, it's a team, the weak and the strong flying together, same speed, same direction, and never trying to out-smart one another."

That was how we learnt to fly, Rodney, Lucille, Jason, Lizzy and myself. Just the same way as all the other kako kids of the jacaranda tree did, from the master flyer himself, the unforgettable old Roy Crow. He was some kako.

All my life I've never forgotten what Old Roy taught us about flying. Some things I remember better than others. The chiseling story, for instance, never left my mind. Anytime I flew behind another crow I remembered Old Roy and his wise words, and made sure I kept my speed right to avoid chiseling into the front kako's arse.

So that's the story of Old Roy Crow, the Jacaranda Condominium flying instructor, always looking for the 'silver linings' in life. One wing fractured and one wing firm, Roy with his memories of faraway places and the long lost splendour of our beautiful world, who perched on the top branch of our tree and watched in contentment as the world rolled by. He had his memories, of where he had flown and what he had done. He always said that was enough.

"Memories, boy, that's what life is all about, if you have them, treasure them, boy, for they'll last you as long as you live."

Time had certainly blunted his ability to recall all his adventures and he lost some of the details as the years went on. But, there was still enough left in Old Roy Crow's mind to make rainbows of what he remembered.

He came alive when he had a few of us new kids to teach what he knew best - how to fly - and to tell about the sky beyond the jacaranda tree. And then he went back to his place aloft, hopping from branch to branch with his one bent wing and one good wing, to wait for the next batch to come.

Old Roy, he certainly was some kako, now long gone but still well-remembered for his 'boy' talk and silver linings and chiseling and peeling to stay with the wind, and the way he taught us to dive and pick dry leaves, imagining them to be papaw pieces.

05

The Train Crow

The Seasons changed and the world was warm once again. Our days confined to the Jacaranda Condominium were coming to an end as we grew stronger and our little wings filled out with fine black feathers. Our flying improved, and was soon almost perfect. We couldn't wait for the sun to rise. As soon as the inky sky showed traces of light on the sun-rising side we would wake and join the other crows in the morning 'kakaphony', that greeted the day, everyone cawing in happy harmony, busying ourselves with the business of flying out for the day. We, of course (that's Rodney, Lucille and I), had permission only to fly around the jacaranda tree, and that was exactly what we did; like most other obedient little crow children we strictly followed the rules laid down by our elders.

It wasn't long before we received our clearance to go further.

"Remember, children," that was Alice at her stern best - "no going far, and no doing things beyond your age. Just fly to the beach, enjoy what you see, and come back safe."

So began our venture out to the world we'd never seen before. Of course Mama Alice led us out the first time, to make sure we knew where to go and, even more importantly, how to make the return journey home to the jacaranda tree.

After that, we went out flying every day, unless the skies were weighed with rain. We would leave in the cool of the morning and fly slow and easy to where the river flowed to the sea. It was a small river and a very big sea, and the sand where they met was all biscuit gold. The waves spread right along the coastline and slithered like thin white serpents to crash on the shore. It was hypnotising to watch, how they came and how they splashed, and how parts of the serpent jumped up to the sky spraying water everywhere with a "*slosh-shoosh*" sound that Rodney tried to imitate. Though the beach extended on either side as far as our eyes could see, we had permission only to go where the river coursed through the golden sand and emptied itself into the foamy blue sea. This was the path we were permitted to fly, from the Jacaranda Condominium to where the two waters met. The rest of the sky was a 'no-fly' zone. Mama Alice drew her boundaries tight, and we never dared to break those demarcations which were clearly and firmly drawn.

"Obey, children, obey!" We heard it a thousand times and we knew there were another thousand coming. "Go to where the water is, perch, enjoy the breeze, and fly back home," her instructions were very clear, with precise limitations.

The beach was a captivating place to be in the early hours. It was the favourite haunt of many a kako, especially those fond of eating fish. The boats came there in the morning loaded with their night catch, and the easiest thing in the world was to find a piece of fish or even a whole small fish, and start the day on a full stomach with a seafood breakfast. Those fish-loving crows did that every day.

We, of course, were there to enjoy the action. Mama Alice always fed us before we left home, so there was never a need to go hunting for food. We had our favourite spot atop a train station that gave us a crow's eye view of everything that happened. We watched the boats coming in, and we watched the trains going out. We saw fish being unloaded and trains filling up with people. We watched boats, we watched trains, we watched everything, while the salty breeze ruffled our feathers as it passed by.

The most fascinating sight was the blue world, the blue of the water so perfectly matching the blue of the sky that it was difficult to figure out where they joined. We would tilt our heads and look at it all upside down which made the sea the sky and the sky the sea. No difference.

Sometimes we picked up some food too, nothing fancy, just a left over fish meal that one of those fish-loving crows couldn't finish or some little dead fish that the boatmen didn't bother to collect. Sometimes we would meet other kakos who were visiting our beach from more distant places. They were young like us, kid crows, perhaps also with strict mothers like Mama Alice, who had given them permission only to come to the beach for an outing. They were all there to test their wings and to make new friends. Sometimes they came over and spoke with us. If they were males they preferred to talk to Lucille, and if they were females they were too shy to talk to Rodney and me. But we spoke to them. Rodney was great, he could make friends anytime, anywhere. He was very clever with words, and he had a dozen or more well-practised opening lines.

"When did you come?"

"Where's your home?"

"Do you live far from this beach?"

"Can I get you some breakfast?"

He rotated his questions from day to day, depending on his mood and whom he was addressing. That's how Rodney broke the ice. Or he would charge into the fray head-on and ask a pretty crow her name right away, always making it a point to say "Wow! That's a lovely name," even if the name in question was anything but, and sounded like a train hooting.

Those were the best of mornings; flying to the beach, watching the boats and trains, meeting some congenial kakos, using Rodney's openers to make friends, chatting a while, and getting back home safe and sound.

Victor Crow was the master of the train station. He loved trains; he had often gone in them to distant places and switched trains going the opposite way to return to his favourite place, the train shed by the sea. He didn't like condo life.

"Too many kakos and too much noise." That was his explanation if you cared to ask and he was in a mood to answer.

I think this staying away from tree condominiums had more to do with what he loved. That's why he made his home in the train station, from where he could always see his beloved trains.

"I can even drive them!" He would brag to us. We knew better but pretended otherwise. He was a nice old crow, and we didn't want to hurt his feelings.

"One of these days I'll take all of you on a train ride. We can go far away and come back before it gets too dark." Victor's invitation was very tempting. We longed to accept it, but we were not sure what Mama Alice would say. Or perhaps we were.

"What train ride? Are you crazy? Nonsense!"

That was what we expected. Surprisingly the answer was a lot milder than that. She knew Victor Crow quite well, everybody knew Victor, the train lover, and that tilted the scale in our favour. The first round we lost with a firm 'No', but that was always the norm with Mama Alice. She placed a well-calculated value on anything she gave away, and needed a little bit of coaxing and pleading before she would even consider a request.

"Keep pestering your mum, my dearies," Victor always had his own terms of endearment. "One day she'll melt and we'll ride that train."

It took a good week to get the final approval and I think Granny Vini too added a morsel in our favour. Lucille was her favourite among the kako kids, and Lucille had pleaded with Vini to intervene.

"You can go, children, but remember: I'll kill and barbecue that Victor Crow and throw his carcass on the rail track if anything happens to you."

We kept her allusions to barbecues and Victor Crow's body lying on the train track strictly to ourselves, and told Victor the good news. We didn't want him fretting about being charred by Alice.

To Rodney, Lucille and me who'd been only flying from the jacaranda tree to the beach and back, the train ride was a miracle. Even now I can remember every tiny detail about it exactly as it unfolded. I still often go back in thought to that train, to re-live every moment: how we rode, what we saw, how we talked and how we laughed. The train shed is gone now, completely demolished and replaced by giant concrete blocks where no one, not even a crow, can, or would care to land. The trains are no more, they run underground now, in dark tunnels with only dark walls to see out of the windows. And even Old Victor went missing a long time ago disappearing from sight, much like his beloved trains.

But I have the memories. I can still fly back in my mind and be at the shed in a flash, to see the trains crawl out hooting their train calls, and to sit with Victor and hear him talk of train rides to the once upon a time beautiful places to which he'd been. Oh! Victor Crow, you were some train Crow!

"Children, the trick is to know where you're heading." That was Victor explaining train navigation.

"We first pick a nice train and figure out which side the sun is on. Then we ride that train till the sun comes above our heads." That was part one of his navigation instructions.

"Once the sun is well and truly up, we fly out and get on a train going the opposite way. That's how we come back to the point at which we started." He stretched his beak at us to emphasise how sensible his plan was, and we nodded our little crow heads as if to say: "All clear Victor dear. Over and out."

So off we went, that momentous morning, Victor, the three of us, and three other crow kids he had invited. There was Navik Crow, Yanik Crow, and a little ruffian called Dylan Crow who couldn't keep his beak shut and yelled all the time in excitement.

"Let's go, dearies, let's go and see the world, let's see where these trains will lead us!"

With these adventurous words, the train lover flew up in the air and landed on a slow-moving carriage. And so began our train party; led by Victor Crow and followed by Rodney, Lucille, Navik, Yanik and me, and of course that painful, loud-mouthed Dylan.

We sat in a box, a big box carriage with no one in it except two cows who were eating semi-dried hay that was scattered loose on the train floor. The cows looked at us lazily and went back to munching. One of them had a bell around her neck and every time her head turned, the bell chimed as if to tell the world the cow's head was turning.

"That's the stupidity of those Great Ones, to hang a bell on a cow's neck. That poor fool doesn't know whether she's a church or a cow, and may even think she is a church kak-kak-kak!" Victor gave a rough laugh.

The cow mooed, and we weren't sure what she'd said. We figured it was a greeting, from the way she sounded. Little Dylan returned the moo with a piercing yell. The cow looked hard at him, frowned, and shut up.

We soon forgot the churchy cow as the train picked up speed. Everything we saw was new to us. Trees went flying past along with telephone poles and even houses. We watched them go. Off and on Victor tried to explain things but we hardly heard him. The noise of the train drowned his voice and we only knew he was shouting at the top of his voice.

"Watch everything, but keep an eye on the sun. We have to get back!"

I watched the sun very carefully; I didn't want to go to Victor Crow's funeral, if Victor was killed by Mama Alice because we'd missed the sun and lost our way.

We passed crowded smoke-filled towns and then railed through less crowded, less smoke-filled towns, before coming into a serene valley sleeping in peace. The air changed, the sky changed, and the land changed: everything was different here, quiet and tranquil as if everything had stopped moving to make the beauty last. We rolled on, breathing in the sweetness of fresh air and hearing only the wind and the chirping of birds. We thought we had rolled into heaven.

"No, children, see!" Old Victor pointed out.

"It is almost like heaven," he said. "Any place is heaven on earth as long as it hasn't been touched by our GREAT FRIENDS!"

Did he sound disappointed? No. Disgusted? Yes.

The train went into tunnels that were dark, a darkness that lasted a long time. We came out to the light again, between big black boulders dressed up with patches of light green moss. The mountains beyond the boulders were green too, a deeper green, carpeted with trees, and from where I was perched, I couldn't see their tops. That's how high they were stretching up to the cloudless sky. The train slowed down as we went curving around the mountains. Victor immediately took credit for this.

"I told them to go slow so that you can enjoy the scenery, get a better view of everything."

Sometimes the wheels' song changed, when we were going over wooden bridges with rivers flowing beneath. These rivers were wide and strong, even a bit wild: they flowed as they pleased, as if nothing could stop them. On the banks we could see long, log-like crocodiles basking in the sun, lying on their stomachs on the crusted mud, deaf to the world and everything in it, just letting the world go by.

"Look at them Crocos, children!" Yelled Victor Crow over the noise of the wheels.

"The Great Ones copied that from the Crocos, this lying in the sun and staying quite still," he explained.

"Of course the Great Ones lopsided the whole thing, and messed it up, as usual. They broke up the Crocos' act and gave it two names: 'sunbathing' and 'meditating'," the Train Kako added dryly.

"It was all copied from our Croco friends. The seemingly wise ones go to the mountains to meditate and the not so wise ones go to the beach to lie still, where they get fried up nicely."

He had a smirk on his face. He nodded his head and repeated to himself a tuneless song which went something like this:

"Sunbathers on the beach, meditators on the mountains
Sunbathers on the beach, meditators on the mountains
Copied from Crocos lying in the mud"

It seemed a ballad composed on the spot.

The moment we passed the bridges, the wheels changed to another song, as the train picked up speed and rolled along again on solid ground. We kept a sharp look out, swinging our heads from side to side to catch everything we passed. Along the track were hundreds of little bushes with hundreds of little flowers, mixed multiples of rainbow hues. Hovering around them were swarms of butterflies and other insects, thousands of them, exploding silently in a wild frenzy of colours so magnificent that only God could have painted them. Everything around us was so pretty, every sound so sweet, and every scent so fresh that if the Jacaranda Condominium was home, this certainly was heaven.

Once we stopped over a bridge, we didn't know why, but we were glad the train had come to a halt. It was a sight to remember, a moment to freeze in time. Victor rolled his eyes and tilted his head.

"I told them to stop!" His gesture seemed to say.

We remained motionless for a while, relishing everything that was before our eyes. The mountains, the river and the sky, could be seen clearly together, going on a long, long journey to meet on the far distant horizon; the mighty mountains, the lazy sky and the hurrying waters, all heading in the same direction. It was just as Old Roy Crow had described in his fairy-tales, an indescribable far away place.

I think even Roy would have lacked adequate words to accurately describe what we were seeing from that stationary train.

"You've got to see it to believe it, Boy," he might have said, "untouched by people who only know how to ruin it!"

"How true, old Roy Boy," I murmured to myself, "how true." I believed you then, and I sure know now.

The train sped on again and Victor yelled to be heard. The cow rang her bell and Navik and Yanik tried their best to keep that noisy Dylan quiet. The sun was crawling slowly along, and was almost at its dizziest height, frying the day. The train came to a stop at a big train shed.

"Come on, dearies, time to switch trains," called Victor.

We nodded our good-byes to the cows and flew off, following our leader. The bell cow raised her head, the bell sounded, Dylan Crow yelled, and I smiled to myself remembering what Victor Crow had said about the cow thinking that she was a church.

Our return journey was on a much slower train, and we had a better chance to see everything that had rushed past us on the way up. We even saw little Great Ones waving to us, standing by the rail track. They must have known we were going to see the world for the first time.

The slow train stopped in many places, and every time it stopped we flew off to explore the surroundings. We stayed close to Victor Crow all the time, because he was keeping an eye on the train.

There was always plenty of food in the train stations, those buffet bins had not been cleared. They were filled to the brim and overflowed with food.

When the train hooted, we flew back to our carriage.

"I told them to hoot and let us know so we wouldn't miss the train." Victor seemed to know everybody and everything about trains.

The sun was going down on the far horizon when we got back to the point at which the river met the sea, to our beach and to Victor's train shed. The sky was awash with a riot of orangey shades and the world was getting ready to say good-bye to another day. A few kakos still hung about, pecking at the fish that were left in the boats. Some were just loitering around, having a last kak-kak before flying home.

Mama Alice was there too, waiting for us.

We didn't get to sleep that night until very late. We were so excited that we twittered for hours telling Mama Alice every detail. We told her about Navik and Yanik and the ruffian Dylan, and the cow with the bell who thought she was a church. We described the mountains and the rivers and the impossibly blue skies, and marveled at it all. Mama Alice was happy to see how excited we were.

"You've seen the world as we knew it, children, as it used to be. All that has changed in many places now, since the Great Ones came."

She'd done some train rides in her time and seen some places too, but not as we did, with the best and the greatest champion train crow ever, our Victor.

It was a long time later that we heard what had happened to Victor Crow. He had switched from trains to ships. Some seemingly wise crow had told him he could do the same with a ship: go one way, change, and come back the other way in another ship.

"Simple, so many have done it. It takes a much longer time, though."

So he went, our Victor Crow, never to return. Maybe he went too far, lost his bearings and flew to another ship that went somewhere else. Maybe the ship itself had lost its way? Who knows? All we know was that there was no more Victor Crow at the train shed.

Every time we flew near the beach and saw hooting trains, we remembered Old Victor Crow, the train lover who gave us our first sight of the breadth of the world. Then he went away, and we somehow knew he would never come back. The train shed was not the same without him.

We hoped that wherever our Victor was, there would be plenty of trains around. That's all he needed to be happy.

06

Football Matches and Romances

One thing we kakos had in plenty, was time. As we grew up to be young and strong with powerful wings to fly the 'blue yonder', we came to realise what a wonderful life we had inherited, just by being kakos. This 'nothing to do' syndrome and its companion phrase 'all the time in the world', were a great combination that contributed unconditionally to a carefree and fun-filled lifestyle. We had time to waste, you see, we were like being retired, before we even worked a single day, relaxing, enjoying life, and flying around without a care in the world. Man! Didn't we revel in it! We made the most of each day that the Good Lord had so kindly gifted to us.

"Just find some food to keep you strong and healthy, see the world and enjoy it." That was Mama Alice's simplified version of a contented kako existence.

"Remember what I taught you, don't pretend, and don't try to be too smart or too wise. Be the crow you are, just as God made you, and you will have no problem."

That's exactly what we did with our days. We didn't have to do much to enjoy everything that was around us. Food was no problem at all, there was plenty of it, and we had so many things to choose from. For that we must thank the Great Ones: they wasted so much, cooking or buying a lot more food than they could ever eat, and throwing everything that remained into our buffet bins or simply on the ground, all over the place, so that we kakos could have a feast.

No problems with food, no problems with accommodation. So what, you might ask was the problem? Truth be told, there was no problem at all. Our primary task in those days was to enjoy ourselves. Life was always kept simple in the kako world which is why, perhaps, it was such a wonderful thing to be a kako. No wonder Mama Alice called us God's chosen ones; we certainly were, and of that we had no doubt at all.

It wasn't long after we started flying that Mama Alice let go completely. That was the custom in the Kako Kingdom: build your nest, lay your eggs and hatch them, keep predators away, raise the kids prim and proper, teach them life, and teach them to fly. And then, when their little wings are strong enough and their little minds are wiser, let them go.

That was the expected norm from a kako parent.

Wise Alice raised us fine, that's for sure, and what was most meaningful about it all was that she did it purely out of love for us.

She never asked for anything in return.

That was Alice, our Mama Alice or Wise Alice, whatever she was called, she was perhaps the most wonderful mother a kako could ever have, or maybe the most wonderful mother anyone anywhere could ever have.

As I was saying just a short while ago, the seasons changed, the days became warm, and the skies became crisp and clear, bluebell blue with just a few fluffy clouds drifting from one side of the sky to the other. The sun took an extra long time to make its day's journey, and the rains too mostly kept away. Ever so often a delicate shower would fall, as if designed solely to keep things cool, give us bluer skies, and even more time to enjoy ourselves between each time the sun came up and disappeared again on the far horizon.

These were good times, as good as I can remember, times of fun and frolic during which we flew to our hearts' content, met old friends and made new friends, chit-chatted and exchanged visits. Altogether we had a crow-ball of a time.

That was when Rami Crow first came to the Jacaranda Condominium.

She was from a place not very far away. Rodney and I had been to that area and it wasn't much of a location to call home. Ours was much better. Rami always pretended she was from somewhere else, maybe to maintain an aura of prominence for herself. We knew better, Rodney and I, though we chose to pretend otherwise.

I'll say this for her, she was pretty, a bit toffee-nosed, but pretty. There was more to Rami Crow, by the way, than looks alone: the spice of the slice was her dancing. She didn't fly, she only danced. That was her main attraction and she knew it. Rami the dancer would go from one Jacaranda branch to another, swinging her hips, nodding her head, and flicking her eyes from side to side, all to a perfect rhythm and all for the benefit of us young kakos, who took bets on which one of us would win her.

There was another little secret to Toffee-Nosed Rami that she had difficulty hiding. Rami couldn't sing a note to save her kako soul; never mind songs, she couldn't even sing our anthem, the "Kak-Kak" we were born with. That was too much for her, and when she tried, it was always out of tune.

Rami could dance like a ballerina and was pretty as a picture, but it stopped right there; her singing was always tuneless and flat as a stale chapatti.

Mooshu Crow was our cousin, I don't know how this cousin business came about, but Mooshu always claimed he was our distant relative. He lived far away and often came visiting us when the days became warm and long.

"It is a far place to fly from, takes a long time, not so easy to come visiting you!" Mooshu always liked to pick up a few credit calls.

"It's not at all far, boys." That's what Roy Crow said when he heard Mooshu boast about his long distance flying. Roy had been everywhere, seen everything, and knew it all.

"Boy, I tell you the trouble with that Mooshu fellow is he doesn't go as the crow flies."

When Roy went metaphoric, he reverted to his favourite 'Boy' talk, but he knew his facts.

"He zigzags, and he loafs, and he loiters. No wonder he takes a long time to go a short distance. And then he tells himself he's flown a long distance."

We never believed 'cousin' Mooshu but we could see that all this big talk about flying far, like most other boasts he made, were mainly for Rami Crow's benefit. Mooshu had seen Toffee-Nose Rami dancing and prancing and she had made a big impression on him. Mooshu was just an ordinary kako and didn't have much with which to impress a female. He had no fancy cards with poems on them or red roses picked from other people's gardens. He could only talk of what he ate and where he flew, that was the entire repertoire of this loafer kako trying to impress his lady-love. And so, Cousin Mooshu had to exaggerate a little, to get Toffee-Nose to notice him!

Unfortunately for Mooshu, Rami wasn't the easily-impressed type either, and required much more than where a silly crow had flown to get her going. But our Mooshu was a persistent fellow, the 'never take no' type and he kept at it, always trying hard to be around Rami and making use of every opportunity he got to sweet talk her with his travels and what he ate.

"Things change, my friends," Mooshu Crow would say hopefully. "Things always change."

Though at first he didn't seem to be getting anywhere with his wooing, we could see that Mooshu's romantic efforts were slowly filtering through the hard armour Rami Crow pretended to possess and, I should add, very loudly professed.

Even among us kakos, there was always hope that love might be blind. Otherwise what would a pretty thing like Toffee-Nose see in a loafer like Mooshu?

"I'm going to ask her out," Mooshu told Rodney and me. "This meeting and nodding and hello-goodbye stuff won't work." He surprised us by adding, "I want to take her on a date and romance her till she falls head over heels in love with me."

That was the plan. The problem was getting Rami to agree to it. This is where a little kako friendship can come in useful. Rodney volunteered to have a chat with Toffee-Nose to pave the way to the date, leaving the rest for Mooshu to complete.

Mooshu's date was all about taking Rami to a football match. We kako lads loved going to the Great Ones' football matches, not that we knew much about how they kicked the ball or why they blew a whistle. Neither did we know or care who won and who lost. But we liked the sights and sounds, and the singing and the shouting. It didn't stop there either, as most of the time they fought one another too, hundreds of them throwing bottles and sending hot dogs flying; it was all very entertaining, like an open-air theatre comedy, a real major mess-up of the Great Ones that we kakos watched with glee. That was the football part.

And then, after the match there was the food part. We loved all the fancy food the Great Ones left behind, all over the place; we kakos always had a feast. The buffet bins regularly overflowed, and half-eaten packets of food were scattered everywhere; and if you loved potato chips the football field was the place to be. All shapes and sizes of chips, in all possible flavours, spilled under almost every seat. The aftermath of a football match was always a wonderful chip-feast, fit not only for us kakos, but for anyone with a taste for chips.

Those match places were big and packed with Great Ones (who I think paid a lot of money to get a seat). For us it was free, of course, we would fly in, perch anywhere we liked, watch the match, eat to our hearts' content, and fly home.

Going to a football match was a highlight of kako life.

We all knew the Great Ones would be playing a very big match on a certain day in the evening. From morning, people were arriving by train and by car, or simply walking there: they packed the streets. People were everywhere and the whole town was filled with football men we had never seen before, men in all colours and all shades, most of them waving multi-coloured flags. There were posters too, on every wall of every street, big coloured ones, and even though we couldn't read the letters, from the pictures on them we knew they were all about football.

It was to be a great day with a great celebration, but the Great Ones as usual were behaving as they always do, like thoroughbred fools. They were drinking and shouting and fighting long before the match even started.

Mooshu knew he couldn't hack it on his own to fix the date and get a nod from Rami. He needed someone to soften Rami Crow before he made the final bid. She was no easy cheese; by gender alone she was one of those who love to refuse for the sake of refusing. It was Rodney's role to talk to Rami, to tell her how nice it was to go to a football match, and watch them kick the ball, hear their shouting, and finish the date by eating from the Great Ones' well spread buffet. That was the paving the way required; such was the master plan.

I think our Rodney did a good job in getting Rami interested in the football match. Mooshu Crow had only to put the finishing touches.

We didn't really see how the date-paving went, but we saw, soon enough, that cousin Mooshu had succeeded.

They flew out that afternoon, Mooshu Crow leading and Rami Crow following on their way to the football stadium.

"Those Great Ones make such a fuss about getting a place to sit and watch," Mooshu explained to Rami on her pre-departure brief.

"We don't have to do any of that, we just fly in and pick our seat. We can sit on the green itself and watch from close range, or we can perch on the goal post and get a kako's eye view," said Mooshu, giving Rami the options.

"The problem is, everybody can see us!" He was objecting to his own suggestions.

"Our best bet is to sit where the giant lights are, way up high and above the game. If we perch there, we can see everybody, and no one can see us." Mooshu Crow certainly had more than football matches on his mind.

But Toffee-Nose wasn't having any of that 'way up high and nobody can see us' nonsense.

"Let's go and sit on the goal post, Mooshu," Rami politely declined the invitation.

"Good choice, Rami! That's definitely the best of the two." Mooshu might have been a little disappointed but he back-pedalled with grace.

So, that's how they went on their first date. Mooshu Crow and Rami Crow, two young kakos who sought the excuse of a football match to pick at the strings that tugged their hearts, curious about the possibilities of life, wondering if those strings might harmonise. There's nothing new in all this of course. It is a story as old as the world itself: shared by all and shamed by some.

That evening we saw them return, two kakos flying abreast, almost pasted to each other like the two wings of a butterfly. They fluttered in by the dimming glow of the sun's last rays, just as darkness was cloaking the jacaranda tree and the stars were stepping out with a weak and tentative blink.

The curtains closed on the football date.

Mooshu Crow, reveling in the events of the day delivered a post-date commentary.

"We had the best seats, man, and the best view too, right on top of the goal post." Mooshu gloated. "There were a few other kakos who had come for the match, all on dates, and all with pretty partners, but mine outshone them all."

Even Rami was in a talkative mood.

"The match was nothing much," she declared. "I didn't understand why so many came to watch a few funny fellows kicking a ball." Toffee-Nose was obviously no football fan. "There was this one football man they all liked, a dark man in a bright yellow shirt, with long hair and teeth all over his mouth, and laughing all the time to show them off. They whistled and cheered every time he took the ball. He didn't even kick much, but kept the ball dancing between his legs," she blushed a bit having said that, the metaphor perhaps sounding a bit too saucy for her straight-laced toffee mind.

"I loved the place, anyhow, and the way it vibrated," she admitted. "The best part about it was not the match, it was the colours they wore and the flags they waved and the singing and the shouting." She gave a non-football fan's impression of the day's events. "A few of the Great Ones fought too, as if they had come to a battle."

"But it was very exciting!" And that's how Rami Crow, toffee-nosed dancer, was tamed.

That night, in the pale light of a laughing moon, the three of us sat on a high up jacaranda branch and spoke, Rodney, Mooshu and myself. That's when our cousin whispered to us the essence and the finale to the fairy tale.

"Know something?" he said with a strange sparkle in his eye.

"No. What?" we said.

"I think I'm in love," the loafer conceded.

"And I know she's in love with me too."

He then made a face that lit up better than the moon above, and declared with the certainty of someone who had got to where he wanted to go.

"She told me so."

It wasn't the usual Mooshu Crow boast; it was the truth.

That was how the football match date ended. Mooshu Crow and Rami Crow had made their sacred vows on the football field and had solemnly promised to share their lives together.

It was time then, to build the nest.

07

Some things were sad

As time went by things did change in our lives, but most remained the same in the Jacaranda Condominium. We were getting old, and others older than us were getting older, that was for sure. Young ones were becoming bolder and the old were becoming milder. That's the way with the kako world, a constant rotation of roles, in which the elders move out gracefully, leaving the youngsters to replace them and run the jacaranda show.

Stanley Crow went away one day and never returned. Stanley going missing from time to time was an accepted norm and nobody bothered much about it. Everyone knew he was a loafer who loved loitering and staying away from home for long periods which became longer as he aged. He would disappear off and on, and come back after a few days. Every time he returned he had some very tall stories to tell us. Mama Alice, of course, was never impressed. She always had that skeptical 'Don't I know!' look on her face when Stanley boasted of his heroics. As the years went by, we too began to realise that the truth was far removed from the 'fairy-tales' Stan kept spinning every time he returned home after a few days of tramping with his friends. Even my sister Lucille began to treat Stanley's stories with subtractions and divisions, and stopped asking idiotic questions which encouraged

Stanley in his embellishments. Old Stan didn't mind; he loved telling us what he did, where he went, whom he met and what he ate. Despite the length, breadth and height of his tales, they all ended with how happy the heroes were to get home to their loved ones. Stanley was Stanley, and Mama Alice accepted him for who he was. She never asked him nor did she want him to be anything but just her own Stanley Crow.

"That's what love is all about, children," Alice used to say often in his absence.

"Your father is what he is, and he is not all that rotten. Sometimes in life it is a matter of acceptance." And she'd shake her head and roll her eyes to emphasise her words. "It's all a question of how you look at things." She would pause a moment to let the words sink in. "Seeing something good in somebody is important. That way the rot can be reduced, and some little niceties can be added to make matters better and more acceptable," she would add on a serious note.

"Don't forget it is not only the sun and the moon and the mackerel clouds that make our sky so beautiful, the tiny stars make their contribution too, don't they?" She looked up through the sparse jacaranda leaves at the darkening dome of the heavens, where a few little lights were appearing shyly to adorn the body of black. What she said was true. We too looked up and saw those diminutive dots glittering and making their presence felt in that dark mass.

"Remember, children, he is your father, and he will always be your father, no matter what, that's the way to look at it. The only way there is" she added firmly. It was very clear to us from her tone that she knew who Stanley was, had accepted him, and that was that. I guessed this was love, of the real kind; that must be what Alice felt for Stan. We were too ignorant about love to understand exactly what Mama Alice meant when she said those things about Stan. Oh, it was true that she at times confronted him, showed up his lies for what they were and forced him to admit he wasn't the great kako he said he was. Maybe she did that to make us realize that it's not all that important to have a hero as our father. Her esteem for Stanley was not because of his heroics, but rather for the fact that he had been the one who built the nest with her, and brought us into this beautiful world. *That* was what needed to be appreciated. That was what really counted in Wise Alice's eyes and she drilled it into us to ensure Old Stan had a revered place in our little kako minds.

It took me a long time to really know what Mama Alice meant when she spoke to us in defense of Stanley Crow. By then, I too was a grown kako and had seen the world was mostly made up of shades of grey. Everyone's a hero and everyone's a villain at some time in their lives. Some are more hero than villain and others more villain than hero, and no one knows how to keep the score. I wish I had spoken with Stan and told him I understood all this, or just him. As with most things in life, I was late to this realization. Stanley is now long gone and I have no way of telling him that I love him for who and what he was, or despite it.

Come to think of it, Rodney, Lucille and I, we never had boastful stories about our father to tell fellow kako kids. At times we even had to hide or give excuses for things Stan did which the jacaranda clan thought to be silly or stupid. So we made up stories to show our friends what a great a kako Stan was. It mattered when we were young, but not anymore. I guess growing up has made us all realize that life isn't only a matter of black and white.

We have to be grateful to Mama Alice for always making sure Stan kept his place as the head of our family.

She never failed to tell us who fathered us and gave us life. Though Mama Alice seldom praised him in his presence she always had some nice things to say in his absence.

That last time Stan went away, it took many days for us to hear some news about him. This time he had been away much longer than was his norm and no one had seen him in his usual haunts where he used to hang around. We weren't worried exactly, but I did feel, during those days, Mama Alice was a bit more concerned about Stan's long absence. As the days began to add up, I often saw Alice in a pensive mood, scanning the sky as the evening lost its light and darkness cloaked our world. There were many kakos passing overhead, flying back to their homes. She watched them go past the jacaranda tree, but there was no Stan.

He never returned.

When the news came, it was brought to us by a passing kako who told us he thought he had seen someone like Stan. This kako had happened to be flying by the jacaranda tree, when he heard some bird mention Stanley, and that he was long gone, for much longer than usual.

"I think it was your Stanley," the informer kako told the Jacaranda crowd. "Better go and see, and make sure. The one I'm talking about was a bit of an old kako and he fits the description of your Stanley Crow. He was lying on the ground, near the meat market." The passing kako hesitated a bit, then added stoically: "He was dead."

We all flew down to the meat market to see Stanley. It was him alright, lying lifeless near a ditch where the butchers came to urinate. The sight was indeed sad and it became sadder still when Mama Alice broke down and started to cry.

Stan had been the love of her life, he had shared her nest and raised us, doing what he could do to make us all happy. Maybe at times he spoke big and maybe he wasn't the best around, but he was Stan, neither perfect nor the worst, just a journey bird amounting to little, but still a kako of the jacaranda clan who had lived his life in the best way he knew how. That was Stan.

Mama Alice loved him and he loved her. It mattered little who loved more, who loved less, who ranked higher in the "who loved best" competition. There was love, and there was the nest and there were the three of us; that was good enough for Mama Alice to shed her tears and say a grieving lover's goodbye to old Stan, the great Stanley Crow of the tall stories and cheese stealing escapades.

The funeral experts from the Jacaranda Condominium flew in to arrange everything. They started with a very loud choral session of our "kak-kak" that lasted through the entire event. Stan's interment was well organised and was conducted with all the traditions of a proper kako wake. The entire Jacaranda Condominium was present along with many more kakos from other nearby trees who had known Stan and Alice. We three flew around our father's dead body, stayed close to Mama Alice, and sang the wake songs of the kakos at the tops of our voices. Everything was laid out in perfect detail by the funeral experts and everything went well, solemn and simple: a fitting tribute to our dear departed Stanley Crow.

A kako end had no wreaths, no monuments, and no superfluous mourning like the Great Ones usually had. No bands played, no funeral marches and no one gave speeches about the dead kako. No money was spent on a fancy casket to rot with the body and be eaten by worms. I still think we kakos do things pretty much right, when the time comes to let go of our loved ones. We paid our last respects to Stanley, left him where he rested and flew off to our homes. Stanley was dead to the world and he lay motionless by the drain near the meat market. Soon enough, we knew that some butcher who came by to urinate would see Stan and kick him into the gutter. Just a worthless carcass of a crow in the ditch, that was how the Great Ones would have seen him. They knew the rains would come, fill the drains and carry the body away. Stan would drift to wherever the water went, maybe to the river, or perhaps to the sea, and then from there to oblivion.

Stanley Crow had lived his life and died. His kako soul could have been anywhere, we had no way to know. All we knew was that Stan was no more. True, his crow corpse was lying in the drain, waiting for the rains, but surely, we thought, his crow soul had to be somewhere else. Perhaps flying around in space until a new place was allocated for it as the Good Lord thought fit.

If God had a place for everyone, then there must have been a place for Old Stan too. Maybe heaven was not only for the Great Ones. That's what they liked to think, but we had hope there was a place there for us, too.

Surely, God would not have created everything and everyone in this beautiful world, and reserved a special place for only the Great Ones to enter whilst the rest of us just disappeared. No! Of course not. That could not be right; even our little kako minds could clearly see that this story about a special place in God's Heaven with a sign up saying "Great Ones only admitted here" was just a fabrication. Heaven couldn't be a place for them only. If truth be told, I am convinced and remain so to this day, that there must be kakos wearing halos in heaven, their black wings turned to the white of the saintly, flapping and soaring about among the chosen who made it to God's special domain. Maybe there are a few kakos who've done even better, and have made the grade as angels? Maybe some could have been so good they may have even been promoted to the rank of archangels.

I doubted very much that the Good Lord who had looked after us so well would have simply forgotten our Stanley Crow. He wouldn't have let his soul waste away in a meat shop drain where butchers came to urinate.

Maybe in heaven he has become the usual Stan and started telling his stories again.

08

Croco Martin

We met Croco Martin when we were young birds, and at a time when we didn't have many friends other than our kakos. Rodney, Lucille and I were just beginning to know the world a little better, and making slow progress learning what lay beyond the path from the Jacaranda Condominium to the beach where the river met the sea. Once we had mastered flying that stretch, we started exploring further, and began to move outwards in different directions. Our first foray from the known to the unknown was to fly along the river from the beach to places from where we could return before night fell. Here, old Victor Crow's sun method worked well for us. We flew till the sun came over our heads and then turned back, just as he had taught us when riding trains. That way we always had enough time to return to the beach before the night took over the day. Victor had taught us the timing part of these journeys. The navigation part was handled by Alice and Roy.

"Just follow the river, children. Do that and you'll never get lost." Those were Mama Alice's clear instructions. "All you have to do is to fly along the river and when you want to come back, just turn around and follow the river again, and you'll be back at the beach. From there, you know the way home." Super simple navigation by Alice Crow!

"Go and ask Roy, he'll tell you more."

"Take it easy, kids." That was Roy Crow. He always took things easy, looking for silver linings in anything and everything.

"So, what if we get lost?" I asked.

"Just find some tree and stay the night in it," said Roy. "You can find your way back when the sun comes up." He added: "Best of all, by doing that, you'll have the whole night to think of some convincing story to tell Alice."

Everyone around us knew how strict Mama Alice was, and the way she put her 'no nonsense policy' into action when dealing with us.

"You see, boy, the river flows to the sea from the mountains: that happens everywhere." Roy explained adopting his usual 'boy' talk. "There is no river that flows from the sea to the mountains."

"Why not?" That was Lucille, with her usual questions.

"Why not?" Roy gave Lucille a 'you shut up' look. He didn't like interruptions.

"That's the way it is, rivers flow from mountains to the sea, and not from the seas to mountains." Roy dismissed Lucille.

"But if you want to fly along the river, just watch the direction. First fly against the flow of the river, and when you want to return just fly the opposite way following the flow." With these words, the Grand Master navigator concluded his lesson, simple and safe. That's how we knew a sure way to navigate, and to find our way back to the beach.

We picked a clear day without a cloud in sight to make our first trip along the river, solo.

We flew under a blue sheet of sky with the river beneath us, keeping our eyes glued to the curving waterway. It passed through the town and then moved away from the houses and shops and the bridges that spanned it, to areas that were less populated. The further we went, the fewer the houses and still fewer the Great Ones. After some time, we were flying over places that had no houses at all.

"Look Kakiyan!" Rodney yelled, while flapping his wings hard to keep up with me. I was always fast in flight.

"Look Kaki, the river's going in one direction and we are flying in the other direction." He was excited. "It's just as that Roy Boy described it."

I saw it too. At the start of our journey, when the river was wide, it wasn't that prominent in which direction the water was flowing, but as we flew away from the beach the river narrowed, and we could see that the water was moving rapidly in a direction opposite to the one we were flying.

"It's always the same, children, never doubt the Master who created everything in this planet, from the mountains to the beach. That's how the rivers flow, never the other way." I remembered how Roy Crow had described it all.

We stopped off and on to rest a bit and then flew on. Food was never a problem for us kakos as we eat anything and everything at anytime. That is a great advantage we have over the fussy creatures who only eat meat or survive strictly on vegetables. I have never seen a cow that ate meat, or for that matter a dog that ate grass. It's stupid, when you think of it, to be that choosy. As for us, we have never gone hungry. That's the blessing of being a kako for you.

Once, we stopped at a place where there was a bridge across the river. There were a few Great Ones hanging about doing nothing, sitting on benches and eating bananas. It was a good place for us to stop too, as there was a bin there filled with all kinds of edibles that had not been cleared for a long time. We were cautious at first, for we had always been taught to be careful when there were Great Ones around. We circled and had a good 'look-see' as Roy Boy had taught us to do, then landed on the roof of a shop. We waited patiently and watched carefully to make sure there was nothing suspicious about the place. Even then, we kept Lucille on 'look out' perched on the roof, while Rodney and I descended to the ground, tip-toed to the bin, and leapt onto its lid. There was a great deal of food there and we took turns to eat. Rodney first while I watched, and then I, while he watched. We each picked out something special for Lucille, a piece of papaw and a fish head with the body missing, and carried it to the roof so that she too, could eat.

Frequenting unknown places and staying on the ground were not wise ways to go about life. That's something the seniors grilled into us young kakos when they taught us about life.

Rodney and I flew around the shop compound while Lucille ate, just to see what this place was like. It was really just a shop and nothing much else, and the people there were a little different from the Great Ones we knew. A clan of the Great Ones whom they called 'poor'. Now, that is something we kakos can never understand, this poor and rich business. Among us, we're all the same, no kako is 'rich' and no kako is 'poor'. We all have a place to call home and we all have our families, and we all eat and enjoy life in the same way. We were well organised from the time we came to this planet. Not only we, but all the animals and the birds and the fish and the reptiles followed the same system. It's only the Great Ones who are different. They have no idea of equality. We have plenty of it. They fight and struggle to be better than the others. I think that must be how this poor and rich thing came about. Poor shops and rich shops, poor people and rich people, everything they do divided by this line which no other creature on the planet knows or cares about.

Rich and poor, man! That is some division!

Anyway, we stayed awhile and rested, and said hello to a monkey who was sitting on a box with a chain around his waist. There was a horizontal pole fixed at two ends and the monkey's chain was attached to this with a metal loop which allowed him to move up and down the pole and extend himself to the length of the chain. That was the extent of his world, the length of the pole plus the chain added together. It wasn't difficult to figure out who was responsible for arranging that.

He said 'hello', too. He told us his name was Tony and he asked where we were going.

"We're just flying around to see what the world is like," I told him.

"You are lucky, my friends," Tony Monkey said, "I don't want to see the world, but I would be very happy if I could only reach those trees that grow tall there." He pointed to a line of huge trees that stood on the river bank.

"I've been tied here as long as I can remember. From the time I was a very little monkey, swinging around in those same trees up there." His voice was very sad. "I fell, you see. They caught me and they've kept me tied up from that day on."

We felt very sorry for Tony. Lucille's eyes filled with tears when she heard of the monkey's predicament. Imagine losing your freedom before you have even fully known it, and spending the remainder of your life tied to a pole.

Tony Monkey had nothing to look back at, except a few far removed childish memories when he swung from tree to tree living life unrestrained. That was all gone now; the Great Ones had re-designed his life, cornering him with a chain and a pole.

We chatted for a while longer, then said good-bye.

"Go kakos! Fly far and see the world, and one day come back and tell me all about it," he said sighing. With a wave of his hand he gave us a sorrowful monkey farewell as we flew away, traveling once again along the river in the direction opposite to the way the water flowed.

We'd seen crocodiles before. I think I mentioned it, the time we took a train ride with our friend Victor Crow. Yes, from a distance they had looked like logs, lying motionless on the river bank. The crocos we saw this time were different, and as we took a bend in the river we came upon a beautiful sandbank jutting into the water. On it were a few crocos, silent and asleep, basking in the sun.

"Let's stop and say hello to them, Kaki," says Rodney.

"Why not? We've never associated with crocos before," I said. We glided, came low, and landed right next to a very big croco, the biggest of the crocos on the sandbank.

He didn't even bother to say hello, just opened one eye, looked at us, and went back to sleep.

Three little kakos were of no interest to him. We moved around, going even closer to the other crocos, but no one said hello. They just opened their eyes, looked at us, and closed them again.

There were some others too, on the sandbank. I think the entire river community was present because that sandbank was a beckoning place: sun, sand, and the river's tiny windswept waves lapping up to the shore, caressing it like lovers do. Long-legged birds, short-legged ones, long-beaked and short-beaked birds, they were all there, strutting daintily, hop-skip-flying, moving from place to place along the sandbank talking to each other. Some were even walking on the backs of the sleeping crocos, pecking and picking up buggies that had made their homes in the crevices of the crocos' thick skins. We thought that was great! We'd never eaten croco buggies before, so we asked those birds whether the crocos would mind if we did the same.

"Go ahead," said a cocky-looking long-beaked bird. "Just make sure you don't peck at a croco's eyes. Go to that big fellow, Croco Martin, he doesn't talk much but he's ok."

We hesitated, uncertain about just making our way over and helping ourselves to the croco-back buffet. That's the way we were brought up by Mama Alice, never to take anything for granted, and to always be polite.

Rodney tip-toed up to the head of the big croco and asked: "Hello, Mr Croco, can we pick the ticks off your back?"

Croco Martin said nothing, he just blinked at Rodney, so we daringly took the blink for a 'Yes'.

From then on it was croc-stomping fun. The three of us had a field day eating buggies off Croco Martin's skin. We walked all over him, from his head to the end of his long tail, picking out ticks. They tasted great, too. He didn't even seem to mind when Lucille walked over his face and nipped between his nose and his forehead.

We spoke with everyone there, especially the long-legged birds. They told us they never went anywhere, but stayed among the reeds by the water. They laid their eggs there, and brought up their little ones, who never went anywhere either, not wanting to leave their beloved sandbank.

"It's nice here. There are only us birds and the crocos, and no one comes to disturb us," said the talkative bird who had spoken to us first.

We stayed a long time on that sandbank. The sun was almost coming over our heads, it was nearing the time for us to fly back home.

"Don't worry, we'll be back," Rodney said. "We like this place and the buggies sure taste good."

"Come again, and bring your friends, too." The invitation was a warm one.

We said 'so long' to all the birds and the crocos of the sandbank, and prepared to leave. We walked over lastly to Croco Martin, whom we all liked the best of all the sandbank crocos; a croco of few words, but warm in friendship. We walked right up to his face to take leave.

"Bye big croco, bye Martin Croco!" We nodded our heads and said our good-byes to our new found friend. He mumbled some sounds in a language we didn't understand, but by the glint in his eyes we could tell he was happy to have met us.

Then he mumbled a bit more and by the tone of his voice we knew he was asking us to come again.

We had a stop to make on the return journey, to say hello to the chained monkey. He was so lonely, and we thought he'd like to talk to us again, so the three of us flew back the same way we had come and stopped for a short while at the bridge. We told our monkey friend about the sandbank by the river, the long-legged birds and the big croco called Martin who was now our friend.

"It's great that you can fly anywhere you like," said Tony Monkey. "I wish I had wings, but then, I only want to get to the trees over there."

That night at the Jacaranda Condominium the talk was all about our journey along the river. We started telling the story to Mama Alice, and a lot more kakos came along when they heard our excited voices. There was Rami and Mooshu, Granny Vini, Dincy crow and her daughter Lizzy, and many, many others. Even Roy Crow came down from his high perch to hear where we had been. He took full credit, of course, for the excellence of our navigation.

"Just as I said, wasn't it Kaki? Go against the flow of the water and come back following the river, as simple as that."

I think Mama Alice was very proud of us that night. Especially when we told her about the new places we'd seen and the new friends we had made. I think she was proud we had made a friend of Croco Martin, for very few kakos have croco friends. But she gave us most credit for spending time with the monkey who was chained from his waist.

That was Alice of course, always sad for the ones harmed by the Great Ones.

Flying along the river to the sandbank and meeting Croco Martin and other friends became a favourite pastime of ours. Every time we made that journey we never failed to stop and say hello to our monkey friend, Tony, who always welcomed our visits. He kept repeating to us how delightful it was to break the monotony of his life and chat with us.

Then one day he wasn't there. We were happy, thinking Tony Monkey must have broken his chain and escaped. We flew around his 'high trees' expecting to see him joyfully leaping from branch to branch and laughing at the top of his voice. But he wasn't there. There was no trace of him.

We had no one to ask and no way of finding out what had become of Tony Monkey.

Our friend had always said that he only wanted to go to those trees and live there unchained and free, as he had done as a child monkey. Maybe Tony Monkey changed his mind and went somewhere else, or maybe something else happened to him. Tony had been chained for so long, I suppose anything was better than that pole-dictated circumference of his life.

Maybe he went away, maybe he died, either way we hoped he was free and untethered.

As for our friends on the sandbank, they became well known to us, and we to them. But Croco Martin remained our favourite. He was always there lying on the sandbank, basking in the sun. He loved it when we walked along his back and pecked at ticks.

Little by little we came to understand his mumblings, and he never failed to thank us for visiting, and tell us to come again. We even took other kakos from our area on the journey along the river to say hello to our bird friends and to proudly show off our bosom pal, big Croco Martin.

He was always pleasant to anyone who came with us. He greeted them and said nice things in his mumbling language, though half the kakos couldn't understand him.

"Any friend of Kaki and Rodney is my friend," he liked to say.

He'd purposely leave out Lucille, and then when he knew he had hurt her feelings, he'd open his wide mouth to laugh out loud, and add: ".....and Lucille's friends are my best friends!" That was his idea of humour, croco style. He said little, but meant much.

That was our dear friend, Croco Martin, big and strong and getting lots of sleep on the sandbank.

09

Gabriel Crow - The 'Yako Kako'

Even among the kako clan there were a few undesirables who deviated from the path of peace and joyful living and made a nuisance of themselves to their kako brothers and sisters. Though they were not many, there were a few of them off and on, painful kakos who caused irritation from time to time to others in our condominium. Such offenders were known among us as 'Yako Kakos', the trouble makers in an otherwise serene and orderly crow community. Of course, they didn't get far with their misbehaviour, at most a little misconduct before the complaints would begin to roll in. The Judge Kakos would step in to stop them. Yako Kakos would first get a warning, a stern injunction to stay away from trouble, which let them know they were now marked and monitored. The subsequent offence was punishable by a sound beating, under the orders of the Judge Kakos, carried out by strong, young kakos with very sharp beaks. The scoundrel would be pecked unmercifully till he bled, and the punishment repeated as needed, to make the lesson stick in everyone's memory.

There was, of course, some shame involved in this meting-out of kako justice, since the entire proceeding was carried out in broad daylight, within sight and hearing of all and sundry. The pecking kakos flew around making as much noise as they could and pecked the hell out of the delinquent. They made such a racket that even the Great Ones below stopped whatever they were doing to witness the administering of kako justice. If that didn't convert the culprit, the final, disastrous step would be banishment from the home condominium. It was a life time ban: no parole, no arrangements for rehabilitation, no hope of pardon, and definitely no return. They were not welcome in other condominiums, too.

End of story in the kako community.

Yako Kakos punished in this manner were rendered homeless. They spent their nights in solitude, balancing precariously on electric wires, courting death every time they fell asleep. Now, that was living on the edge, balancing on live wires on a daily basis, separated from the comforts of kako condominium life and the warm conversations of the kako community. We all knew, too, that these kako criminals didn't have long to live. A miss here, a miss there, a nod-off in their sleep was all that's needed to execute the death penalty. They went the way of those stupid night bats who flew low, swung low, touched two wires and ended up barbecued, dangling dead till 'thy kingdom come'.

The Judge Crows, being the serious types they were, didn't tolerate any nonsense. They met on given dates, choosing nights when the moon was full - as rounded as a cheese ball and glowing through the clouds – so there was plenty of light for everyone to get a good view. We kakos knew all about variations in moon sizes, and we marked the passing of time by the waxing and the waning of the moon. As the moon increased, kakos with grievances they wanted resolved would prepare their cases to bring before the Judging Courts on 'Big Moon' Day. On that night, we kakos slept little, if at all. We would gather in an orderly manner in the Jacaranda Condominium, take our places, and wait without a hum or twitter to hear the goings on of Judgment Night.

The supreme judge of our condominium in my time was Justice Samuel Crow, who had been in the judging business for a long time and knew everything there was to know about it. He was a very wise and dignified crow, an elder of our community, and had a reputation for undisputed integrity. Everyone knew of his ethics, and no one dared question anything he said about law and order.

"What they have down there is no justice at all." He occasionally voiced his opinion in a frank and 'matter-of-fact' manner on the subject of the Great Ones' judging practices down below.

"They wear fancy coats and comical false hair, and bang a gavel incessantly, but that is all," he once said. "There's no justice, it's just big talk with big books and bigger buildings. For offers of big money they change their judgments when someone powerful is entangled in the net."

"I've seen a lot and heard a lot in my time, and I can tell you, there may be law down there, but there is little justice."

Judge Sam Crow had spent a lot of time near the justice houses of the Great Ones from the time he was a crow kid. The nest in which he was hatched had been built in a large ironwood tree that shaded an imposing building, where supposedly justice was dished out to wrongdoers. From infancy, he had been around this court house and had keenly watched and listened to all that happened inside and outside of the premises.

"As a young kako I almost lived in the Great Ones' courthouse," he said with pride. "I saw everything that took place there. At times I sat right on top of that fancy coated judge, over his head on the roof bars, and gave my sentence to offenders who I thought were guilty."

Samuel Crow once recalled a time when he, with a "kak-kak-kak" had given an unsolicited judgement.

"'What was that?' the Judge asked, looking around curiously to identify the unseen source of the noise that had broken the solemnity of his court. 'Did someone say something just now?'"

"'No, your Honour,' said the legal officer in charge of proceedings. 'It was just a crow cawing on the beams.' The judge looked up and saw me. I too gave him a hard stare followed by another 'kak-kak', and flew out of the courthouse."

Sam Crow had been around, following judges and lawyers and law-breakers alike, and had overheard many secretive conversations between the villains and the venerated on quiet benches in secluded gardens. He'd witnessed some criminal exchanges too, big wads of bank notes wrapped in cellophane, passing from hand to hand surreptitiously like a pick-pocketed fortune, quite unlike what you might expect of men of the law. He'd also heard promises made, oaths sworn and allegiances established, while he lingered around pretending all the time to be just an insignificant crow hanging about in the vicinity. That's how he knew so much about what happened between the so-honest law-makers and the so-called law-breakers.

"It's all too convoluted and clandestine." Judge Sam Crow would say pulling no punches about the Great Ones' legal world.

"They take a long time, often many moons and sometimes the passing of many seasons too, to decide what is right and what is wrong, as if that's such a difficult thing! By the time they make their decision, everybody but the plaintiff has forgotten what the case was all about. We, on the other hand, charge a kako, give him a fair trial, and either sentence him or free him then and there."

He ran a super-efficient kako court.

We all knew that Samuel Crow was a kako who knew the law from beginning to end. Bar none, all our judges were the same, knowledgeable and honorable, all senior citizens of the condominium, and they could never be influenced or bribed to pass lesser sentences, as happens so often in the judiciary of the Great Ones. Kako justice leaves no room for buying and selling pardons: the law has been laid down, so the law must be obeyed. Whom you know and who spoke to whom – well, those simply never arose on the agenda of a kako court.

We had a Yako Kako called Gabriel in the Jacaranda Condominium. In his younger days he had been warned several times for minor offences, but obviously had not yet learned his lesson, and had graduated to bigger crimes as he grew older.

I'd always felt a bit sorry for him, though, because I knew something about his background. He'd had the misfortune of growing up in a garbage dump as an orphan. This happened after the nest in which he was hatched broke loose and fell out during a severe storm, leaving Gabriel and his two sisters inside a large open garbage bin. The next day a truck came, collected the garbage, and drove off to deposit everything in a garbage dump. Gabriel survived the calamity, but unfortunately not his sisters.

That's how he ended up living in a garbage dump all by himself.

Mama Alice would remind us that Gabriel had missed out on parental love and that all he knew about himself was that his name was 'Gabriel' – that was all he remembered about his infancy. The name Gabriel didn't do him much good either, because as soon as the cheeky young kakos in that area heard he grew up in a garbage dump, they promptly christened him 'Garbage' which they later shortened to 'Garby'.

Anyway, whether as a result of this accident of birth or not, Gabriel had always been a loner. He found his way to the Jacaranda Condominium, but he made no friends there. He didn't know much about the opposite sex, either. He'd never had a steady companion, and he developed the rather dangerous habit of directing 'come-hither' glances at every female kako in a shiny black skirt.

Well, of course kako husbands didn't like that. One thing was sure, this was a crow who had been warned often, and pecked often, but had never learned his lesson. The judges themselves were losing their patience, and were waiting for an excuse to catch him and banish him, once and for all, to rid our condominium of this incorrigible Yako Kako. Garby Crow was a marked kako, surviving on the last fragments of patience and tolerance the condominium dwellers, rather grudgingly and out of sympathy for his past alone, scraped together in his favour.

Rodney and I first became aware of the breadth of this Yako Kako's tricks when our sister Lucille was late flying home one evening.

"Hello, where've you been?" Rodney asked.

"At Uncle Gabriel's singing class," she said. I noticed that her gaze didn't quite meet Rodney's eye.

"Gabriel Crow? I didn't know he was giving singing lessons," I said.

"Oh, yes, he is! Uncle Gabriel says I have a beautiful voice and he's training me to take part in next month's Condominium Concert."

I realized then for the first time that our little sister Lucille had been growing up into a pretty good-looking lass, while Rodney and I had, it would appear, been looking the other way. Shining, black feathers, brilliant bright eyes, a cute way of pecking up her food daintily without spilling any ….Brothers don't notice these things where their sisters are concerned, I suppose.

I don't trust that fellow, Lucille," I told her frankly. "He's a Yako Kako, you know."

"Yes, I've heard all those stories and I don't believe them. People shouldn't call him names, anyway, when his name is Gabriel. *It's* so *unfair.*

I knew better than to press the matter. Lucille took after our mother, and she didn't like being crossed. However, I knew Gabriel Crow's reputation with the ladies, and had heard plenty of tales about his unwanted approaches to female kakos who stayed home, while their husbands were flying around looking for food to feed the brood.

At the time, I felt he was more mischievous than rotten, though I knew from reports that the line was sometimes blurred. He seemed to have his own way of looking at life, which nobody understood. Perhaps that was his problem, a weird appearance and weird thoughts, and never conforming to the norms of the crow world.

He was lazy, too, and seldom flew out looking for food. He often stole from others, ate and fattened himself. Gabriel was also just plain annoying often, his favourite trick being to fly to the top branches of our jacaranda tree and shit on any kakos below, purely to irritate and upset them. Though he was reported sometimes for his misdoings and received punishment from the Judge Crows, he managed more than a few times to get off scot-free, wriggling himself out of situations either by pure luck or by the silence of a flighty kako female who enjoyed flirting while her husband was away. Gabriel's smooth talk and winning smile might have concealed a more sinister villainy, but I didn't want to judge him too harshly.

Nevertheless, I thought I'd better keep an eye on the progress (or otherwise) of the singing lessons he was giving our Lucille.

It was a good thing I did, because it wasn't long before Garby Crow decided to give my sister some advanced voice lessons, which required her to stay even later at her singing class.

Flying home one evening, I decided to take the route along the sea shore. There had been a disaster there some years before, when two trains had collided and one of them (a passenger train filled with commuters), had toppled killing scores of people. The Great Ones believed the area was haunted by the spirits of the dead and they didn't go there if they could help it.

We kakos, of course, didn't believe any such superstitious nonsense. Rodney and I sometimes picnicked there with our kako friends, and we never saw a single ghost. The wrecked train was still there and we enjoyed flying in through the windows and out again, chasing one another through the broken window panes, confident that no Great Ones would disturb our games.

Anyway, I was flying home enjoying the sea breeze, when I happened to look beneath me. I saw a most unusual sight. A ring of kakos were gathered on the ground beside the engine of the wrecked train, around fifteen or twenty of them, and they were dancing with excitement. Something was going on at the centre of the ring. I swooped down to get a better view, and right away some of the birds spread their wings and flew off. 'What were they up to', I wondered as I flew in closer, that couldn't bear the scrutiny of a fellow kako?

I was curious to find out. As I flew lower, I detected an unusual movement on the ground beneath me, and looked down to find an agitated flutter of black feathers in a hollow at the centre of the ring. It was a female kako, pinned to the ground by a big black crow, who was holding her down, and ignoring her appeals to him to let her go. I folded my wings, dived downwards, and jumped on him immediately. He was much bigger than me, but he was so intent on what he was doing that he didn't see me coming. All his friends had fled, so no one gave him a warning. I pecked him as hard as I could, till he released his victim. It was only then that I realized who she was: none other than my little sister, Lucille. I didn't waste time asking her what she was doing so far from home. Explanations could wait, especially as I could see that her pretty black silk dress was in tatters, and that both her wings had been twisted backwards, as if she was being readied for roasting. I turned on her attacker, and had another surprise. It was Yako Kako Garby Crow, the impresario of the Jacaranda Condominium.

"Out of here, you," I screamed. "And *stay* out! You will be hearing from me."

I saw Lucille safely home and said nothing about the incident, then or later, to Mama Alice. But the next morning, after Mama Alice had left for a Mother Kakos' meeting, Rodney had gone to watch football at the Great Ones' stadium, and we had the nest to ourselves, I put some tough questions to Lucille.

"What happened to your singing class?" I asked. She burst into tears.

"There is no singing class," she said. "There's no training for the Concert. It was all a lie. Uncle Garby calls what he was doing to me a 'Training Session' because it takes place in that train. It's his idea of a joke. He called a bunch of his friends together to watch the

'Training Session', learn his methods, and then take turns 'training' me."

I'm not often speechless, but this account of Garby's behavior robbed me of words. When I got my breath back, I asked Lucille: "Is there anyone else he's treated in this way? Any of your friends?"

"N-no," Lucille sobbed. "He told me I was a special pupil, requiring extra expert attention from him, due to the quality of my high notes. So I was the only one he was 'training' for the Concert. I thought it was an honour to work with him."

"Oh, Lucille," I said. "I warned you he was not to be trusted. Why didn't you come to me? I'd have checked him out for you."

"You'd have told Rodney and Mama," she said. "I wanted the Concert to be a surprise for the family."

Did I turn Gabriel Crow in to Jacaranda Security? Well, I thought a lot about it, you can be sure, but I decided with difficulty to keep it quiet. Lucille had suffered and was ashamed. True, I was very angry and disappointed to stay silent, but it was better that way without my sister becoming the laughing stock of the Jacaranda Condominium.

Lucille, too, pleaded with me many times not to pursue the matter as it was very embarrassing for her. It was clear that she did not want the Jacaranda crowd to get to know what happened at the train track. She was also petrified of the consequences if Mama Alice came to know of the shameful saga.

Garby Crow didn't dare to venture anywhere near our nest after that, and Lucille sadly gave up her interest in singing.

That was a shame, because she really did have a pretty voice for singing.

All went back to normal after this incident till Gabriel once again pushed his luck and went a little bit too far.

He'd been telling the young ones in the condominium stories about why Granny Vini flew up to the top branch and sat with Old Roy Crow, and sometimes even stayed overnight with him. It was an undisputable fact that of late, Vini Crow was getting herself up there and spending a lot of time with Roy. But that was their business and theirs alone, and there was no reason for Garby Crow to slander them, especially making up tall tales and mumbling to the young kakos about what Vini and Roy were up to at the jacaranda summit.

A formal complaint against Gabriel was lodged, and since the Yako Kako was on his 'last warning', the matter was deemed very serious. Slandering others was not something we kakos did, spreading ill of fellow kakos was considered a serious crime in our world.

"What's wrong with him? Is he unhinged?" That was Dincy Crow, questioning the sanity of criminal 'Garby'. "Is he trying to be like the Great Ones? Always talking ill of others?"

We all know how Great Ones love to think and say the worst about their neighbours.

"So what? What's wrong in Granny Vini spending time with Roy? Maybe they're elderly, they're certainly not young anymore, they may not make nests, lay eggs and raise kids, but everyone needs company and if it comes with a bit of love, so what? Is there an age limit to love?"

That was Mama Alice firing "a broadside" in defence of whatever it was that Granny Vini was doing with Roy Crow. She was always broadminded, generous and practical. I doubt she would have been equally pragmatic in the case of Garby and the 'training' sessions he gave Lucille. Broadminded or not, Mama Alice would have murdered Gabriel Crow if she ever came to know of what he did to our Lucille.

Granny Vini's case was taken up. It was she who had complained, Roy didn't care. He probably looked at the silver lining and was pleased that someone was taking notice of his geriatric romance. Vini was not so easily pacified. She felt she'd been insulted, and doubly so, for Garby had been telling all these amorous tales to young kakos barely out of their nests, and they with mischievous glee had been giving Granny Vini knowing glances whenever she passed them by.

Gabriel's crime was cardinal. He'd been speaking ill of others, and the Jacaranda Judges meant business.

The case didn't take long, it was short and sweet as one might say. Of course Garby was given a chance to defend himself, but he had no defence. The little ones were all there (delighted to be allowed by their strict Mamas, once in a way to stay up late), perched in a row on a jacaranda branch, summoned by the judges as witnesses for the plaintiff. They all, bar none, nailed and crucified Garby Crow well and truly by repeating in open court what he had said to them of Roy and Granny Vini.

The judges learned that Garby had not only slandered both these elders of the condominium, but had painstakingly exaggerated everything in the telling and had related all this to the little kakos in 'gloss-finish' detail, using the sauciest language possible.

The crow judges sat solemnly and listened carefully to everything, and whispered among themselves before Justice Samuel Crow, their chief, delivered the verdict. Gabriel Crow was found guilty of slander. He was sentenced to banishment for life from the Jacaranda

Condominium. True, he'd got away with a lot of things before, escaping with a sound pecking every time he erred. But slander was a serious crime in the kako world.

I was present in Court. Hearing the case, I was glad I hadn't made Garby's outrageous treatment of Lucille public by reporting it. Lucille had learned a timely lesson about life, even though her singing teacher hadn't.

That night a dejected and saddened kako softly stole away, flying into the darkness by the pale light of the fading moon, perhaps in search of a temporary lodging on a telegraph wire. Gabriel Crow was found guilty as charged and his crime proven beyond a reasonable doubt. Kako justice had prevailed. Samuel Crow and his fellow judges had delivered a sentence the offence deserved: a lifetime's banishment for speaking ill of others and damaging the innocence of the next generation.

I distinctly remember some crow (I cannot recall who) saying at the time of the hearing how strange it was that slander was so common in the world below. According to his information, speaking ill of another person was not even considered a serious offence among the Great Ones!

Old Roy and Granny Vini kept up their friendship and saw a lot of each other. I guess it was love at last sight, that's what everybody in the Jacaranda Condominium said. Theirs was almost like a final attempt to make the most of what was left of their lives.

Mama Alice, as always, was right, of course. What after all, did age have to do with loving someone?

10

Kako Sport

It's a little bit embarrassing to talk about what we
young kakos did for sporting competitions. You'll
soon see why.

But we had an excuse for it. We couldn't just get up
every morning, fly around, eat something, and get back to
sleep every night without some extra-curricular activities,
could we? That would have been too dull. We needed
some excitement too, and some form of competition
to bring out the best in us. We all enjoyed the challenge
of matching our wits and what-nots against those of
other kakos. Well! Among crows there aren't any football
matches, wearing multi-coloured sporting jerseys, and
kicking balls around in a green sports stadium, to the
cheers of other kakos. We don't run races at the firing of
a gun either, nor do we jump into rivers and swim to find
out who is the fastest. No crow knows how to hit cricket
balls, or bounce, bounce and shoot basketballs like those
big Blackos do, jumping high and flying through the air.

Still, even we needed a little competition, to flare up our
wills and match our wits, to participate in some event just
for the sheer enjoyment of it. Unfortunately, there were,
and I'm sorry to say, still are very limited avenues in the
kako world for this type of entertainment. We certainly
can't compete in the looks department: we all look alike,

there are no extra 'handsomes' and no extra 'beauties', the Good Lord took care of that himself. Neither can we get one up on others by owning something special, for we own nothing. We wear no clothes we can show off, or fast cars we can drive, or boats in which we can sail around the world demonstrating our wealth. The only things we possess are our homes and they too are exactly alike, with the same conveniences: just a corner in some large tree as we had in the Jacaranda Condominium. Equality, while mostly a blessing, can occasionally border on boredom.

That's how our need to jostle, spar and announce winners and losers ended up in the great tradition known to kakos as 'shit shooting', a sport invented a long time ago, long before I came out of the egg, and practised wherever youthful kakos congregate. It is a contest all young kakos take part in whenever they need excitement: simple, effective and fair to all. A Champion Rectum Ranger is chosen by shitting on or nearest to a Great One below. No foul starts, no handicaps, or any such nonsense. Who needs handicaps, merely to shit? Who needs to call 'foul' when everyone can see plainly where the shit falls? The contest is a simple matter of perching on a high place and blasting off on Great Ones passing underneath. The winner is the one with the greatest number of shit-hits; he is named the 'Rectum Ranger Champion' of the day. There's a scoring system, of course. A head shot on a Great One is worth twice what is earned by a body shot; and any shot that hits a target full on the face is considered the best, meriting five times the value of a head shot. All quite fair and easy to follow.

Full face shots are hard to come by. Any player attempting one must plan carefully, practise good timing and make perfect directional calculations. Most times, 'full face shots' demand good team work to accomplish. One kako perched on a branch of a tree or a lamp-post would aim his shit to hit a Great One below, while his partner waits patiently ready to fire. As the first bullet slams the target and if the Great One so assailed is stupid enough to look up to see what had happened, that's when the second kako would let go with a well-aimed shot straight to the face to splash crow shit all over the unfortunate's nose and mouth, chin and cheek, and sometimes on the eyes too. Face shots represent kako shooting at its best and many a young kako teams up with a like-minded partner to practise his technique in order to master the art of blasting a face. Patience, regular practice and commitment to the rules of the game, that's what brings results and guarantees success.

As for the targets they choose, it could be anyone, from ragamuffin to royalty. Competitors could shit on a prince or a pauper, or for that matter, on a pope or a poet. No wonder there's no one among the Great Ones who escaped being blasted by crow shit.

They'll tell you if you ask them. They've all had their baptisms. We owe no gratitude to the Great Ones. They have never been our friends. They mock us for our appearance. 'Black as a crow', 'dark as a crow', 'ugly as a crow', 'common as a crow' - such epithets have always been intended to taunt or ridicule us, and never uttered in praise or even in mere acceptance. Shitting on them is one of the few ways we manage to even the score, chipping off a smidgen from all the wrongs the Great Ones have done us. That's how and why the kako shit shooting competitions have become a very popular international sport among the entire crow community in the whole wide world.

As in any sport, players must practise in order to improve their skills. We would practise all the time and had our favourite places in which to train. There are many life-size statues of eminent Great Ones, standing proud and arrogant all over every town and they make perfect targets for shit-shooting practice. All we had to do was to find one erected under a tree, pick a branch above it, get ready, aim and let go. Of course we missed a lot and shat all over the place, that's why we needed the practice. And as we improved, we managed to hit all 'bulls-eyes,' straight onto the head. This is why almost all the statues of 'so called' greats among the Great Ones are caked with shit.

Even statues that stand in the open without an overhead canopy of trees or roof are at risk. The best kako shit-shooters can score hits while flying, and back then, there were many of us who excelled at that, experts, so to speak. Of course it took a lot of practice, to fly, aim, correct for the wind and the speed at which we were flying, and to still hit the mark. Statues that stand get the same treatment as their tree-shaded companions, standing pompous or sitting bumptious in granite, stone or marble. Under trees or in the open air; they are all full of shit, crow shit.

Those Great Ones, many of them politicians must have owned the world in former times and basked in the glory of temporary power, but that was all gone now. Their current status was to be grossly ignored by the very people who had erected the statues, and the only attention they received was some wayward kako shit on their heads from an unknown crow practising to become a champion Rectum Ranger.

Well! We practised with statues, but the real thing involved firing at live targets, some of them in motion and some stationary.

Our favourite locations for shit-shooting competitions, were the street lamp-posts in the vicinity of the jacaranda condominium. These lamp-posts were tall and straight, bent slightly towards the road, providing enough room for us to perch and enough height to make the sport worthwhile. One lamp-post (a favourite with Rodney and me) stood right under the Jacaranda tree, with a bus stop nearby, and on the opposite side of the street was another lamp-post erected next to a red pillar box. Both were places frequented by Great Ones, places where they stood around as if waiting to be shat upon.

Competitors divided into teams and competed against each other, the Jacarandas against the Mimosas (when we were kids there was a large Mimosa tree near the pillar box - another kako condominium - and the young ones who lived there were our friends.) The Mimosa team was led by Adrian Crow. Now this Eddie (that's what his Mama called him) was always up to mischief. He was a very good shit-shooter, no wonder he was made the captain of the Mimosa team. Eddie had a curious way of flying: he flew in a straight line and only turned to the right, never to the left.

"Maybe he's a right-thinking fellow!" That's what old Roy Crow said about Eddie Kako's odd way of flying.

Adrian's mother, Ashley Crow, was a tough one. She had always taught Eddie to think right and do right, as everything to her was right, right and right. Eddie, being an obedient kako kid listened to his mother, and appeared to have extended her 'right' philosophy to everything he did, including his flying. He only turned in one direction. When he wanted to go left, Eddie turned right and flew the full three quarter circle to go left.

Inevitably, he came to be known as "Right Turn Eddie", the champion shit-shooter from the Mimosa Tree Condominium.

Our shit shooting matches always started in the morning, when the roads were very busy with many Great Ones walking about, arriving to post letters in the pillar box, standing at the bus stop and chatting away with others, while trying to board buses brimming with passengers.

"Ready, steady, *fire!*" Rodney would yell to begin the competition.

"Ready, steady, *fire!*" An answering yell would sound from the pillar box side - usually Adrian Crow, shouting at the top of his voice. There was always an umpire appointed to each side and it was his job to judge where the shots hit, and to keep count. We had our umpire, and the other side had theirs. There was never a need to send our umpire across the road to count the Mimosa shots, or for them to send theirs to the Jacaranda tree to verify the score on our side. Nobody cheated in the shit shooting game, because nobody really cared who won and who lost, as long as everyone enjoyed themselves. We were not like the Great Ones, who loudly herald their 'not to win but to take part' philosophy on billboards all over the world, decorated with those five multi-coloured rings, and then cheat in every imaginable way to become the victors. But no question about it: we needed umpires. Shit-shooting required intense concentration and it was impossible for a kako to shit and count at the same time.

Once in a while we challenged the Pigeons to join us in shit-shooting competitions and then we sent in our best team, selected from both the Jacaranda and Mimosa sides. The Pigeons always insisted on having the contest in one or other of their churches, or in those big bank buildings they lived on – a shrewd move, because it gave them the home venue advantage. But our teams were so good that we always beat them! It didn't matter whether we competed on churches or lamp-posts, we were the undisputed experts at shit-shooting and those cathedral pigeons were no match for our well-trained kako champions.

Shit-shooting was our only sport. Either against the pigeons or among us kakos. Mostly we spared children in school uniforms, the elderly, and people who looked as though they belonged to the 'poor club'. We often waited for our favourites to arrive before we went into action. The leading candidates for our attention were the Great Ones who got off from their big cars to post their mail, mostly well-dressed women wearing smelly scents that reached the high heavens; nothing like a bit of kako wacko on their heads to spoil their morning. That was on the Mimosa pillar box side. We had no big cars stopping at bus stops near our lamp-post but we always had lovers who missed buses, and then missed more buses and waited for no bus at all, just spending time with each other. It wasn't a very nice thing to do, I suppose you'll say, a bit mean and sadistic considering they were probably looking for a cost-effective good time, perhaps the only kind they could afford, standing at bus-stands. But to be fair, we watched carefully and figured out who the underdog was and made sure we shat on the superior lover, just to even the score and bring the level down so that Romeo and Juliet were placed on an equal playing field. You'll be surprised to know what a little crow shit does to peg down the high and mighty.

Once a competition was over, the umpires selected the champion kako, who was then acclaimed as the 'Rectum Ranger' for the day. He flew around certain chosen streets somewhat like the 'victory-laps' of the Great Ones. He was the shit hero of the kakos in the area until he returned in the next competition as defending champion, to try to retain his title.

We had no big-time audiences or cheer squads, nor did we have to fend off other kakos bustling to get autographs from the champions who won. But, it was fun.

The losers usually flew after a match in search of statues in town that could give them some practice.

It was all a matter of crows shitting on those Great Ones.

11

The Thinking Kako

Cameron Crow was different, quite unlike the rest of us in many ways. From his little days he was a bit of a mismatch. Everyone in the Jacaranda Condominium noticed this and spoke softly of little Cameron's tendency to listen to his own music and dance his own steps. 'Normal' crows led simple lives that revolved around the tree they called 'home'. They woke with the sun, passed the day, made the best of everything that was going on around them, and went to sleep when the sun completed its arcing crawl and disappeared on the far horizon.

"There is more to life than the passing of a day," Cameron Crow would say. The rest of us kakos at the Jacaranda Condominium saw his 'more to life' statement as a bit of a joke, and we had a laugh or two at his expense, even calling him 'More to life Cammy' when he was not around. I don't think he would have minded, even if he'd known that we made jokes at his expense. Cameron cruised above mundane kako events and was mostly seen flying out to some secluded, silent place where he would sit with his face to the sun. He sometimes lingered in these reveries for the entire day, looking at nothing we other kakos could see and thinking of things none of us ever thought about.

"Kaki, just look at these leaves on our tree," he once said to me. "They are like us. Each leaf is like a kako flying around. Now, just see, how as the wind blows, some leaves, they fall. But some other leaves don't fall. Why? What is the reason for this?

I had no answer to give him; until that moment, I had never contemplated the falling of leaves. But Cameron had. "The breezes," he told me "are like the troubles we face in day-to-day life. Even the lightest breeze can remove us and make us fall unless we stay strong in our minds."

"That's what we need in life, Kaki! We need to be strong in mind, so that we can accept or reject things that happen to us in the little time we call life."

I may have understood faintly, but mostly I must confess, I didn't.

Cameron had another strange habit (besides asking his friends unanswerable questions). He would tilt his head sideways and remain motionless for a while, and then tilt his head the other way. This we thought very funny. We imitated his movement of the head, and called it the "Cameron Tilt." The gesture became very popular among the jacaranda kakos. In no time, it spread far and wide and became a very common practice in the kako world anytime a crow contemplated anything.

'Want to think? Tilt your head!' became a common expression, and the "Cameron Tilt" was soon a trademarked tradition among all crows of our region.

If you have taken time to watch kakos doing nothing and have seen them tilting their heads, then you can be sure they are thinking of something bigger than eating from a nearby bin. Maybe they too were thinking some strange thoughts as Cameron Crow did, and wondering how to fit them into their hum-drum kako lives.

Cammy never wrote his ideas down or got them published. Who knows, if he had, Cameron Crow may have been world famous today, with a statue erected in his name on some busy, manicured roundabout.

Of course there could have been another side to such fame, too. He might have been persecuted or killed by other kakos who envied him his intelligence and ability to think differently. It has happened before amidst the Great Ones: they are known to have burned and crucified others of their kind who dared to think differently.

I am sure Cameron definitely knew things we didn't know. We kakos were experts on mundane matters, like knowing where to find papaw skins, what time the boats would come up from the sea to unload fish on the beach, or for that matter which bins at certain street corners were never cleared and consequently always overflowing with a delicious variety of food. Cammy Crow's thoughts were different, less tangible, like clouds in the sky.

I remember once it had been raining heavily and we were all cursing about being wet and cold and miserable. We couldn't fly anywhere, the skies were grey and angry with thunder and lightning, and rain poured down nonstop, with drains overflowing and water covering almost the entire ground. We just huddled up and stayed at home, berating the weather.

But not Cammy Crow. He stayed quite still and silent as the showers came down, made him wet through, and soaked his feathers. No complaints came from him, he just accepted it, as you might, a gift. Then, when the sun came out some days later, we all rejoiced, stretched our dripping wings, and bathed in the sunshine to dry our feathers. Everyone was happy the rains had ceased.

"Isn't the sun beautiful today?" we shouted with glee.

"Yes, yes!" everyone agreed.

"The sun's been beautiful every day," whispered Cammy, to no one in particular. "It's been beautiful all the time, if you'd only stopped to look," he muttered.

"That's the problem, Kaki," he told me. "We curse the rain and we cheer the sun. Can we control what they do? No. They are both far beyond our control, and all we need to do is accept what comes to us because we know it will change, from bad to good and from good to bad. It's the way of the world, the way things are."

Occasionally this thoughtful crow would come and spend time with us, listen to the kak-kak-kak going on around him, and make contributions to it with measured words that we could actually understand. It was a rare day when he would share snippets from his thoughts like this. We could have grasped their wisdom if we had taken time to mull over them, but mostly we were too distracted to take Cammy seriously.

Well, that was Cameron Crow of the Jacaranda Condominium: our friend in every way but one: he just wanted to be left alone, to keep his mind free for pondering.

One day I distinctly remember him telling me, "I can't make other kakos think the way I do, Kaki. I want to know more about all that is happening around me."

Sometimes he shared his 'headful' of questions with us, such as why the leaves were green or why the sky was blue.

As for us, we just looked at everything around us and accepted them for what they were. If one morning I woke up and saw the sky had turned crimson, I would still go about my life the normal way, dive out of our nest, find a crust of bread and enjoy my breakfast.

Cameron wasn't like that, he always looked for reasons.

"When we die, something must be happening to us, Kaki."

"Why would I want to worry about what happens to me when I am dead, Cammy?" I asked him. I had often felt there must be some continuation of ourselves after death and spent a few moments here and there wondering where we went, but had always come to the conclusion, 'who cares?'.

"Never mind Kaki. There are some things we talk about, and other things we think about and talk of only with people who share similar thoughts and want to know more. Unfortunately for me, there aren't many who think like me, my friend. It's easy to be like you, but I want to be me, even if people laugh at me and think I am a fool." That sure was a long speech for Cameron.

So another of our talks ended, with no questions resolved. But I appreciated getting a peek into his curious mind. Most times – and especially when speaking to other kakos – he just nodded and kept his thoughts about why the sky was blue and why the leaves were green and why the winds changed directions and went different ways to himself.

Once he told Rodney that anything we ate was very tasty, its tastiness entirely dependent on how you thought about it.

"Yes, Rodney, it's all in the mind."

"Are you telling me that if I eat a papaw skin and think hard enough, it can taste like a piece of cheese?"

Rodney was always very direct. He told me Cammy hadn't answered the question, he had just tilted his head and kept silent. Rodney had tried a "Cameron Tilt" himself then, to see whether his own thinking would change with this cranial adjustment, hopeful he might learn how to make a papaw skin taste like cheese. But there was no magical revelation for Rodney: papaw was papaw and cheese was cheese, and no tilting of his head was going to change that.

I cannot remember many of the things Cameron said to us, because he tended to speak very softly, almost in a whisper, and never raised his voice to emphasise a point as most kakos did, to force their arguments on others. All crows love to argue, and do so in the loudest possible manner wherever they gather. But, not Cameron. He simply said what he had to say, and let it go at that. I think his thinking may have had something to do with this restraint: not shoving his opinions down the throats of others, and choosing not to get angry when his views were not accepted.

He would sometimes say he was happy with whatever he had in life.

"I enjoy everything, and I crave for nothing." Another Cameron gem.

But it was true. I never saw him yearning for anything. When we went looking for good food, he just sat in his branch and ate what was available around the jacaranda tree. He never stole from kitchens or shop windows, nor did he keep looking greedily at the food the Great Ones had on their plates, as we did.

"Food is only to keep us alive, Kaki, the thrill of it is only in our thoughts. The moment it goes into your stomachs, it's all over," he often said. "So what's the big deal in thinking or talking about how good it tastes?"

Come to think of it, he did have a point there. How long does a taste — any taste - last in a mouth? In prospect it could be great, while eating too it could be great, but the moment we swallow it, where then is the taste?

"I sure wish I could meet Whoever created all this and who runs the show," Cameron once said in a serious mood. "I'd make only one request, not to benefit us, since we are already here, but the next batch he creates: to let them open their mouths and eat the wind. No food, drink – except perhaps just water – just make it so they can live on wind. Most of the world's problems would be sorted out with one stroke. No one would have to kill another to eat, no need to watch bins till they overflow or wait for the boats to come ashore to get a piece of fish, or for that matter for the boatmen to spend a cold night out at sea to catch fish to eat. Just open the mouth and eat the plentiful air."

Well, that was some thought, wasn't it! But Cameron didn't stop at that.

"Or, if eating wind is difficult, what if the next lot lost the power to taste anything? They could munch something to stay alive, and not live to eat. So easy, a kako could eat the same thing every single day."

It crossed my mind a few times that the next batch coming to this world eating air or having no taste buds would have a hard time surviving. But I could see his point, so I didn't say anything. If there was no taste, everything in this planet would have to change. The world would only contain wide open grasslands where people could pick and eat all they want. There would be no chickens going abroad in plastic bags, no salmon smoked and stuffed into tins, no pigs made into sausages and packed in cellophane wrappings with fancy labels showing piglets laughing with joy at the thought of becoming a Great One's dinner. Just grass-eaters everywhere.

Cameron Crow had some thoughts that went much deeper than we kakos could comprehend. When our father Stanley died, I remember what Cameron told Mama Alice when we went to the wake. Cameron condoled with Alice saying "sadness is a path to wisdom, and when we face the passing away of someone we love very much, we need to find our inner wisdom in order to achieve peace. It's not easy, but it's the inner wisdom that makes us see the truth in life and death, Alice.

"We must search for it in sorrow. When someone we love dies, something dies within us, and what is born from it is the inner wisdom. We need to use that wisdom to blend our thoughts in such a way so as to overcome the sorrow we are feeling. Otherwise we will remain the fools we have always been, just crying for the dead, without being thankful for the lives they led with us, and understanding how rich we are simply by having known them."

After that I always passed on Cammy's wisdom to anyone who has lost someone through death. I guess it's the truth. There are no variations to the truth, it's just truth.

"You know, Kaki, there is a System to this whole thing…." Cammy elaborated to me.

"There is some Power that runs everything. We can call it by any name, but there is definitely something that runs everything. I am not clever enough to know what that is, maybe God, or maybe gods, or maybe something we know nothing of….. But there is certainly an Unknown, a far superior Factor that knows everything," Camy continued.

"That's why, Kaki, when something sad gives us a shattering blow, everyone remembers their God or Whomever they believe in, and starts pleading. But why? Isn't it better to accept everything and call it life? That

God or Whoever or Whatever that runs the show would have known what was happening and let it happen. So why beg for a change? That's the reason it's important for us to find an inner wisdom of acceptance, give credence to the inevitable, and get on with life. The problem is, we are too naive even to know that we are nothing, absolutely nothing in this vastness that we pass through and think we can figure out the answers to," Camy continued shaking his head.

"At night when you look up through the jacaranda branches and see the stars, Kaki, how many do you think are there? I don't think anyone has ever counted them or anyone even can. Do you think they just came there? No way, Kaki, there must have been a 'Star Boss' with an eye for beauty who designed all that glitter in the sky. If I, with my little kako mind can figure that out, then I must be more of a fool than other kakos imagine me to be," Camy said with a faint smile.

"Maybe I am right, Kaki, or even partially right, or totally and completely wrong the way I figure things out. I don't even know. That is how complicated this whole life is, not just for you and me, but for anyone who steps into this world."

Cameron Crow certainly was a thinking kako, and when time permitted, we the 'run of the mill' wayward crows picked up little wise quotes from him, but in no time we forgot them. I guess we were too busy enjoying life to think of anything else.

Now that I have seen the back of a few more years, I tend to think he was dead right – about sorrow and wisdom. When you suffer, or are sorrowful, you do become wiser. With suffering, you learn to contemplate, when you contemplate, you learn to compromise, and when you compromise you become wise.

"Correct compromising is the real essence of living, Kaki! That is where you learn to scale down and appreciate life, otherwise it is purely a matter of greed." He tilted his head and whispered this to me. As usual it didn't mean much to me at the time. I was young and like all the young kakos I knew everything about everything, except that I was being foolish to think so. But as the seasons changed and I became older, I often thought of Cammy Crow's 'suffering to wisdom' theory and thought it made a lot of sense.

It was Roy Crow who once summed it up.

"Boy" he said, but he said it kindly, "that Cameron fellow is some crow. A bit weird I'd say, but he makes sense if you stop to think deeply enough about what he says."

Roy had been listening to Cammy Crow unravel his thoughts on the meaning of life and he went on to relate to us Cammy's exact words to him.

"There are things in life that are more important than having a good time," Cameron had explained. "It's true we kakos don't have books like the Great Ones below, and there have never been great thinkers among crows to see visions and dream dreams, to find answers to questions and write them down for others to read. But we have done so much better than they. With all their knowledge, the Great Ones have always ignored wisdom, and have kept on being the biggest fools they could ever hope to be." That was what Cameron had told Roy.

The Jacaranda Condominium was a great place. It was 'home' to some unique characters who knew many different ways to make life more pleasant and palatable than it would ordinarily be. Cameron had his special place in it, a bit weird at times like old Roy Crow pegged him, but nevertheless meaningful if you cared to read between the lines.

Cammy Crow's thinking was different. That is a certainty.

12

A Bit of This and That

Lizzy Crow grew up to be a beautiful kako and was eyed by many, including my brother Rodney. Lizzybird and Lucille were great friends and flew around a lot together, mostly making themselves noticeable to young kakos (and always ready, of course, for a little flirting and romance!). Lizzy's mother, Dincy, was very protective, however, and kept her eyes wide open any time a crow suitor came along, singing melodies to Lizzy Crow.

We were all old mates from our flying lesson days. Mooshu Crow and his toffee-nosed Rami joined us at times, but those times were few and far between, as they had their own entertainments with each other to keep themselves occupied. Sabine and Sally Crow were from the tree opposite, the Mimosa Condominium, and they came along with Adrian Crow, our "Right Turn" Eddie, Mimosa's champion shit-shooter. Eddie introduced these two female kakos to our 'clan' and they were good company, game for most things, but as they were a bit on the serious side, we had to watch our language when they were with us. These two got offended and made faces whenever our profanity extended beyond the limits of normal kako expression and touched – however gently – on vulgarity. Other than that, they were ok.

Then there were Blackberry Crow and Moraes Crow, two brothers from a condominium a little distance away, and their close friend, Cyril Crow. Theirs was a flame tree, and their home always looked very beautiful, its branches full of little red flowers that bloomed in all seasons. On a clear day it looked as if a giant had taken a large brush and painted the entire tree in a bright, rufus red.

Blackberry was a strange crow. He was big and proud of his muscular body.

"Know what? I only eat blackberries! From the day I started doing that, I've grown stronger and bigger, maybe brighter too." That was his brag. We all knew he was telling the truth. One day he had eaten blackberries for the first time from a bush that grew in his neighbourhood, and loved the dark berries so much that from then on, he ate only blackberries, nothing else.

Whenever I saw him he was munching a blackberry or had one hanging by its stalk from a talon.

"What if they cut that bush down?" someone asked Blackberry Crow one day.

"I'll find another bush somewhere else, or maybe I'll figure out a way to eat other things, like apples."

That was typical kako thinking: just carry on without worrying about tomorrow. When things change (and not before), consider a new solution. There has always been enough on this planet for kakos to eat and survive, blackberries or whatever other fancy they feel like pursuing.

Our conversations touched on many subjects.

"That boat story the Great Ones talk about so much," said Jason Crow, picking out a topic to discuss at one of our usual gatherings. "Every Great One believes every syllable of it."

"That story's just a lot of lies," Moraes Crow muttered. "A fairy tale as the Great Ones themselves admit." He laughed loud and long sarcastically. "Anytime I hear that 'Noah' nonsense, I know it's going to be one of those tales they fabricate to create heroes. A boat floating around in non-stop rain, with all those couples huddled inside!"

"The Great Ones always make a point of shaming and slandering our kako forefather when they relate that story to impressionable kids in their Sunday Schools," adds Lizzy defending one of our own ancestral heroes. "I know, I've heard them. He was the only hero in that whole rigmarole and they know it."

On most afternoons we passed the time in kako talk. Fly out in the morning, eat our fill, then gather in the shade of some comfortable tree to swap stories and have a good time. Our young crowd consisted of Rodney, Lucille, Jason, Lizzy and me, and sometimes we had other kakos joining us: not many, but a few from nearby condominiums who had become our friends. Everyone had stories to tell - old stories, new stories, fun stories and sad stories too.

Isn't it strange that whenever we hear of something sad in the kako world, it is always connected to the Great Ones and their undiluted savagery? We learned we were not the only ones who suffered the Great Ones' cruelty. It was directed at dogs, cats, rats, bats, birds and even trees. Any living creature occupying some space on the planet was their enemy. What we could never understand was how these Great Ones could be so inhuman to their own kind? Some of the stories we heard horrified us. That kind of cruelty is something totally alien to the kako world.

Anyway, what the Great Ones did to one another, that wasn't any of our business. We had our own lives to live, and the less we spoke of them, the better it was for all of us.

The boat story Jason was talking about at our meeting was from ancient crow history, about an extra-brave kako

127

who made a lasting name for himself in the *Kako Chronicles*. Such narratives have been passed down through the ages. Call them folk tales or history, they were passed from kako mothers to their children, and they in turn related them to their own fledglings in the nest. They were recited with pride, in remembrance of outstanding crow courage.

Jason's story started with the original 'boat people', a very different crowd to the 'boat people' of the present day, who cross oceans to escape from tyranny, and end up behind barbed wires. This was the very prototype itself. According to Great Ones' records, they stayed inside a specially constructed vessel for forty days while outside that boat it rained, rained and rained. The entire world was drowning and everybody who lived everywhere was going to die, swallowed by the water.

Only one man – his name was 'Noah' - knew of this catastrophe beforehand, and he planned to survive the great flood. Without telling anyone else, he built a big boat to accommodate himself and his relatives, and waited for the rain to fall.

"An act of supreme selfishness, in my opinion." It was a quiet whisper from Cameron Crow, who had joined our lively group, as he occasionally did. "It was that boat-builder's duty to alert the whole world – well, his neighbours, at least. I've always thought so."

Nobody challenged Cameron Crow's opinion.

Undeterred, Jason continued on with his story.

Noah it seemed had been working according to a plan of his own, and it wasn't entirely selfish. After he'd installed his own wife in the boat, followed by his sons and their wives, he filled the remaining space in his boat with couples of every creature on earth. It was his idea of a way to re-populate the world after everybody had been drowned by the flood waters of the rain. This man had worked out the entire re-production process, so he and all his couples packed themselves into that one boat and waited for the rain to come. And it did. The rain rained, rained and rained non-stop. The big boat floated, floated and floated and rose with the water level, and saved everyone who was on board.

That was what was written in all the Great Ones' books. Generation after generation, they repeated this incredible story. They even teach little ones in their schools all about the rain and the Flood, and how one man and his couples survived. The story goes on to say that after forty days the rain stopped. The water level came down and the boat was stuck on some mountain top.

The entire world's living creatures had been wiped out by the rain. It was time for the boat people to step out and start reproducing each one's clan the moment they came off the boat.

"Some story that is, elephants in pyjamas and ants in lace nightgowns sharing cabins with tabby cats and mice!" Jason Crow laughed again, more loudly as he finished his story.

"Who would believe such a tale?" Lizzy obviously couldn't believe it herself.

"Believe? They not only believe, the Great Ones even worship the Captain of that boat, and talk of him as if he was a great hero." Jason was disgusted.

"When the rain stopped, everything was silent and watery and gloomy, the sky was a sickly grey with drowned corpses lying everywhere...."

"It must have been very eerie." Lucille was scared just thinking about it.

"Eerie? The Captain and his clan, the entire family were too terrified to even step out, bloody cowards. That's when Capt. Noah asked for a volunteer to go out and explore the drowned world, someone brave enough to go into the unknown. No one came forward. It was our kako ancestor who accepted the challenge and bravely flew out to see how things were."

We all knew this part of the ancient story, but we never tired of hearing it told again and again.

"What about all those supposedly gutsy ones?" Lizzybird asked, adding her bit to the story telling. "What about lions and tigers? Aren't they supposed to be the fearless ones? Or maybe an elephant or a kangaroo, or a hawk that could see far, *where were they*?"

"Hiding inside the boat, where else?" Jason said. "Waiting for our kako to come back and give them the 'all clear' call."

"Some people say he never came back." Everyone pondered the mystery.

"Forty days stuck in a mangy place like that and forty days of non-stop rain, and then you're free to fly, who's the fool who would come back?" Jason asked.

He had a point there.

"Maybe he did come back," suggested Rodney. "One thing for sure, he was the only one who went out of the huge crowd of animals and birds. Maybe he came back, and waved to everyone, saying all clear, and then flew out again."

It was a noble effort on my brother's part to clear our ancestor's good name.

"Maybe it's just another one of those Great Ones' stories," someone said. "The ones they warped to make us look foolish, and promote themselves and their pals as heroes."

The records are all so different from the truth. We all know that part, how they slander our Boat Boy Kako and call him greedy and what not, and say he never returned. Then they sent some idiot of a dove, who came back with a twig and a leaf in her beak! She ended up by making it to the Great Ones' history books as a goody-goody.

Even after all these years they still have that silly dove in their pictures, snow-white and saint-faced, flying with a twig in her beak, getting all the glory whilst the real brave one was our kako hero, who ventured out first when everyone was scared to go. The only thing he didn't do was to bring a silly twig back to the boat.

"Those doves or pigeons, or whatever you call them, have always been prize-winning hypocrites," declared Moraes.

"Why?" That was Lucille, of course, always first with the questions.

"Why?" Moraes repeated rolling his eyes. "Because they're full of shit. That's why. You have to only look at those pigeons who hang around parks and churches." Moraes explained. "When they are down, they'll eat from anyone's hand and when they fly up, they shit on the same people that fed them."

Wonder from where they learned that?

"So maybe the dove came back and the kako didn't, who cares?" Lizzy Crow was on full kako defense mode. "But they all admit our kako was the first to go."

"That's true, no one can deny that."

"You see," Jason concluded, "the Great Ones are so ready to honour the 'firsts' in anything they do, like their man who first went to the moon, or those brothers who flew the first aeroplane, and that Hillary man and the other fellow who carried his bags and climbed a mountain. But when it comes to putting a kako first, they make sure the story is mangled and written in the reverse, not as an honour but as a wicked slander."

"Do the Great Ones really believe all those couples shared a boat for forty days?" Asked Rodney. "What rubbish, they would have killed each other on the first night itself."

"It's the same with that cheese story." Lizzy pulled out another good one that had been doing the rounds slandering kakos.

"Where in this world would a crow get fooled by a fox, try to sing for him and lose the cheese?"

"Every little kid knows that story," she added. "They learn it from their books, and they all think the fox is cunning and we kakos are fools."

"Nonsense," countered Moraes. "He must have kept the cheese on the branch, held it with a claw and told the fox to piss-off."

Lizzy blushed, but we all laughed, the word was a bit off-key for kako profanity, but it sounded real right.

We had all these friends, who sometimes brought along their own friends. Often it was a large gathering of young kakos, spending fun time together. Each one had a contribution to make to the daily conversations, and the essence of it all was very rich and palatable. We were a great lot, the talkative ones and the silent ones and the semi-silent ones (like Cameron Crow) who listened more than they spoke. We had enough to do from sun rise to sun set, and we certainly lived our kako lives to the full.

Whenever the three kakos from the Flame Tree Condominium joined us we always heard some spicy stories from Cyril Crow. Blackberry Crow wasn't the kind to talk much, hardly spoke, kept mostly silent but laughed loud and often, as if to compensate for his verbal limitations. If ever he spoke it was all about blackberries, how tasty they were and how strong and smart you became by eating them. As for Moraes Crow, he knew a thing or two (or three) to make us laugh, saucy things, grown up things. His father had been a great story-teller and he picked up the trend and continued it, but at a lower level.

Cyril was a bit of a peculiar kako, nothing negative but a little different. He was strictly what you might call a 'vicinity crow', never venturing out far from where he lived. He'd hardly been anywhere other than around their flame tree, and visiting us off and on at the jacaranda.

"Why go far? I love it here," he explained to anyone who cared to ask.

"When I am hungry, I fly down and eat, when I'm full, I come back and rest. And when I am bored, I talk to you," he stopped and smirked before adding: "And then I get more bored. Kak-kak-kak!" He'd laugh loud at his own joke and both Blackberry and Moraes would laugh with him as if it were their last opportunity to laugh.

Cyril Crow watched everything, saw everything, and knew everything that happened in the neighbourhood. He often told us some titillating stories.

"It is true," he revealed one day. "It happens in that big house with the red gate." This was one of his favourites tales, and every time he told it, the story was a newer version of the last.

"The Great One goes to work, and another Great One comes like a rogue," our vicinity kako explained.

"Kiss the husband, close the door, open the door and kiss the rogue!" Cyril gave his imitation of the house woman's act. "But I'm telling you it's not the same kiss."

"So what happens then?" Sabine Crow was always one for details.

"Well, Sabby dear, I told you it's not the same kiss." Sabine waited eagerly for more information, so Cyril elaborated. "There's much more passion followed by much more action and then it is one beeline to the couch." Cyril puffed out his chest and flapped his wings to elucidate.

"On a good day, I tell you, if they're in the right mood there's sure to be a lot of action on the couch. Kak-kak-kak," the punch line spat out of Cyril Kako's mouth through an uncontrollable kako guffaw.

For that we all laughed, yes, all of us including Sabby and Sally. It was a good Cyril Crow tale. Rogue lovers and couch gymnastics and the mockery of it all, a common love story among the Great Ones. Adoring husbands leaving their loving wives at home to be spiced and peppered by rogue intruders who stole in and stole out like thieves. Even those who professed to be 'holier than thou' had their little well-concealed amorous secrets, all stocked and locked away from everyone, to be taken out furtively and made into 'grand-slam' performances behind locked doors. All that was kept very private but it was inevitably exposed to roving kakos, who picked up the details from their perches on electric wires and low hanging branches, or from balconies and window sills. Whatever the Great Ones did, publicly or in private, we vigilant kakos were always there to watch the show, to see the illicit mating unfold through wide-open bedroom windows, just as Cyril Crow described.

Such were our daily gatherings and the talk we shared; all for fun and laughter. We flew a bit, stopped a while, ate a bit and gossiped a bit, a simple daily pattern that was easy to follow.

The same thing happened the next day and the next and the next. It was all about living one day at a time, and not having to worry about where our next meal was coming from. The good Lord was there for us, that's what all kako mothers taught their children from the time they were chicks and we remembered the lessons well.

We only had to wake up when the sun coloured the sky, to start enjoying the day. We did it to our hearts' content till the sun moved across the heavens and went over our heads to the other side, to lose itself beyond the sea. Then the skies darkened and it was time to go home and sleep.

That was our day; a perfect gift from the good Lord, given to the kakos of the world who, unlike the Great Ones, know how to value, appreciate and relish it.

It's all as simple as that.

13

What they did to Croco Martin

It was a lazy afternoon and we were chatting, talking nonsense and fooling around, the daily routine of kakos, once we had filled our stomachs with the noon day meal.

Then the news came.

It was brought us by a crow from a nearby condominium, Harry Crow, who described to us what he witnessed a little upriver from our locality.

"They were there with nets and ropes, so many of them!"

Harry was gasping for breath from flying fast, and he said to us: "It's your friend Croco Martin, the big one who comes to the sandbank. The Great Ones came to capture him - so many to fight this one croco - and so many others to cheer them. They were all over the river bank." Harry Crow gasped again, and went on. "Your friend had come to bathe in the sunshine - and the Great Ones were waiting there to capture him."

"Did they catch him?"

"Yes, they did. I saw the way old Martin fought, his jaws wide open, his tail thrashing from side to side, and his short arms and legs trying to break through the net in which they trapped him."

"I watched what was happening, and so did many other kakos, who were shouting as loud as they could, encouraging Croco Martin to run."

"Then?" Rodney asked.

"Once he almost made it," Harry Crow said. His voice was very subdued.

"He struggled hard, and managed to crawl very close to the water, even with that net tangled all over him. Then they put ropes around his head and his legs and held him back. I just couldn't bear to watch it, so I left. It was too sad, to see what they were doing to old Croco Martin."

We flew as fast as we could to find out what was happening to our good friend, Martin. Rodney and I headed to the river, then we turned and flew along the water against the flow, knowing that it would lead us to the area where Croco Martin used to lie, the sandbank and the muddy reeds he called home. The sky was dark with wings, for there were many kakos all heading in the same direction. Everyone who had heard the sad news was flying to the sandbank to see what was happening to our dear old friend, Croco Martin.

There was a very big crowd gathered there when we arrived. We saw them as we turned the bend in the river. There were hundreds of Great Ones there, and like a cheering squad, they were shouting in wild excitement. They seemed to regard the occasion as a big sporting event, cheering and some even jeering at Croco.

Rodney and I, along with some other kakos who had arrived just ahead of us, found a high vantage position from which we could see everything. We all perched on the sail mast of a beached river boat, and from there we watched the tragedy unfolding beneath us. What we could see over the heads of the crowd was a sad sight indeed, a sight I shall remember to my dying day, an innocent and harmless croco being ridiculed by the Great Ones. They never needed much of a reason to act as they did.

The applause was dying down now, 'the contest' was over. It was time for the Great Ones to pat each other's backs, and boast to the world how great they were.

It was a sorry sight for anyone who had a heart to feel. All the Great Ones crowded together around Croco Martin who lay motionless on his favourite sandbank. It was a different stillness to before, when we used to stand on his back, walk about on it, and pick ticks off the scale-covered crevices of his skin.

He was bound from head to toe and his long tail too: ropes going all over his body tied this way and that, held with big knots to make them firm. A large, sturdy net covered his entire body, they must have rolled him over to make it stick tight, leaving him no room for any movement, except to breathe. Croco Martin lay there on his beloved sandbank, immobile, helpless. It would have been impossible to move even an inch of his body after what they had done to him.

It was indeed a sad sight.

It became sadder when he opened his eyes and saw us watching. We sighed silently and our kako hearts nearly broke to see him suffering, perhaps with no idea why they were doing such horrendous things to him. Old Martin kept looking at us, his eyes misty, but even then, too proud to cry.

I don't think I ever saw, and hope I never shall see, a pair of eyes look as sad as our friend Croco Martin's when he was lying there bound, netted and humiliated on his beloved sandbank.

We always knew the Great Ones were cruel, but this was a kind of cruelty that surpassed anything we had seen before.

They continued to surround him: a big circle of people shouting brave words at the defeated croco. For all their boastful courage, they were still scared to venture too near their captured prisoner, so they maintained a safe distance between themselves and the now helpless Croco Martin. Those who had been watching it all from the front row moved out and let others take their places to get a good look at the big croco. It was like a little party on the sandbank, jubilant faces celebrating their victory: Great Ones *versus* Crocos, ladies and gentlemen, and the winners are ....the Great Ones, of course!

Even a van with a musical horn turned up, selling ice cream to the gathered crowd. Don't those Great Ones know how to celebrate?

Out in the water we saw Martin's croco friends floating at a safe distance, watching what was happening on shore with only their eyes and long noses showing above the water. They must have been there from the beginning, watching the events unfold, helpless and angry at what the Great Ones were doing to their friend. The crocos watching would always remember how the Great Ones tortured their old Martin right in front of their eyes.

Would it be a surprise if they hated the Great Ones? Would it be wrong if they chose to remember their friend and take some form of revenge?

The crocos do not have nets and ropes to capture a Great One, tie him up and do the same thing to him that the Great Ones did to Croco Martin. The only way they can wreak vengeance is to use the only weapon they have, their powerful jaws. They can open their wide mouths and bite a Great One who comes to the river to bathe. We all know crocos have done that off and on: bitten off legs and such and sometimes even managed to kill one or two of the Great Ones. But none of that compares to what the Great Ones have done: capturing, torturing and sometimes even murdering crocos, kakos, crawlies, monkies, and others unlike them, from the time they took over the world as masters of us all and claimed ownership of the entire planet and of everything and everyone in it.

As we watched Martin's friends watching him from the water, witnessing the barbaric treatment of their friend, we knew they would surely remember, and do what they could, from time to time, to revenge the capture and torture of old Croco Martin.

To our little kako minds, this felt like justice.

The crowds slowly dispersed, but many more who had heard the news, flocked to the river bank. Some carried sticks in their hands and poked the bound croco with them. Some even used the sticks to lift the skin of Martin's rope entangled mouth in order to see his teeth. Were they counting them? There were a few little boys there (young in years, but old in wickedness) who thought it great fun to throw stones and cheer when they hit the motionless croco. They reveled in ridiculing the fallen. A sad fate to befall a once proud and dignified crocodile who only swam in the river, walked among the reeds and came ashore occasionally to sunbathe and sleep on the sandbank.

"They'll take him to that place where they keep other animals," said a young kako we didn't know. I think he meant the zoo.

"Do you know what they do to crocos there? They keep them in holes with high walls, so that the Great Ones can come and see them lying there."

"Yes, we've seen that," Rodney said. He and I, along with Lucille, had once flown past this place where the

Great Ones keep all kinds of birds and animals. We stopped by some of the cages and said hello to the inmates, but very few responded in any way other than with the briefest look to let us know they heard us. Their faces were expressionless, as if the light behind their eyes had been switched off. Perhaps, being imprisoned when you had done nothing to deserve it, did that to you.

"The crocos we saw were in small square pits, where there were even smaller water ponds in which they were supposed to swim."

"Swim? Swim where?"

"Swim nowhere," retorted Rodney to the kako who had asked that question.

"How to swim?" Rodney was disgusted. "The ponds are so small and shallow, the crocos there could barely fit in them, and that too with their tails sticking out of the water. How could they swim?"

"That's what will happen to Croco Martin," someone concluded. "They'll put him in a tank filled with muddy water and stand behind a wall to watch him lying there with his lights out."

I still remember the anger that rose up in me at the thought of Martin trapped in a cage. He was our friend, and he'd done nothing but swim in the river and sleep in the sandbank when the sun was up. All that was to change for him. No more swimming in the deep waters of the river, meandering among the windswept reeds, dozing on the shore, lulled by the heat and tickled by our feet as we took the ticks off his back. All that would be gone now, replaced with four walls, dirty muddied sand, and a half-filled water puddle, while the Great Ones watched him as if he was an inanimate object in one of their museums.

It was a terrible prospect.

But then an old crow, who'd been around a long time, whispered a worse possibility. He had kept silent during all our talk, but opened his mouth to utter a truth no one wanted to entertain.

"I don't think Martin's going to any cage or any little pond," he said. "He's not that lucky. He's too big for that. They'll kill him and skin him and sell his coat to those places where they make ladies' handbags."

For a moment there was silence: we all looked at each other, broken-hearted. We didn't dare look at poor Martin lying motionless after this revelation. We had heard this before: how Great Ones kill crocos and take the skins off them to make bags for ladies and wallets for men to put their money in, and even stitch shoes from those croco skins. It was terrible. It was disgusting. Handbags, wallets, and shoes, made from someone so harmless, someone so innocent as our dear old friend Croco Martin!

Is there a measurement or scale for such cruelty?

The Great Ones make such a fuss when one of them is injured by a fellow planet-dweller – an elephant, a leopard or a bear - and think all of us are so vicious. Could what we do to them come anywhere near what they do to others, like our poor Croco Martin? Cruelty for the sake of cruelty, that's what Great Ones enjoy doing, to crocos, to kakos, to any creature that walks this planet, and that includes their own kind, their fellow Great Ones.

We waited till everything was over. The Great Ones brought a big lorry, they tied ropes to it, and pulled Croco Martin up. The crowds who had come to see the spectacle gave a resounding cheer as hulking Great Ones threw Martin into the back of the lorry. They clapped their hands and pumped their fists in the air, pleased at how clever they had been in capturing him.

A heaviness fell around us as the lorry drove off taking the road by the sandbank that paralleled the river. We chased after it, shouting our protests as loud as we could, though we knew well enough that our kak-kaks were falling on stone deaf ears.

The few crocodiles who had watched the tragic episode swam down river, trying to keep pace with the moving truck. I don't know why they did this, but it spoke of how much they loved old Croco Martin and how much they hated the Great Ones for what they were doing to their friend.

They watched, and we watched too, till the lorry disappeared beyond the bend in the river, leaving behind a trail of fumes and dust.

14

New Nests and Such

As the years rolled by and the rains came and went, we too became older and stronger and bolder. No more were we kid kakos, but fully-fledged members of the crow community adding our mite to whatever happened in the crow world. Of course, our home was still the Jacaranda Condominium and we ate the same and spoke the same and flew around in the same area with our kako friends as we had always done. Nothing much changed for us as a result of being grown up, except that our hearts beat a little faster when in the company of kako females, and there was that 'Hey! I want you to notice me!' feeling that popped up often when we were in the company of the opposite sex.

The prospect of romance and the possibilities it held must surely be one of life's greatest thrills?

The kako system is age-old, well-thought out and well-respected. There's no compulsion to make life-time commitments to selected partners and then break every rule in the fidelity book. Our system is simple, super simple. You meet someone, you love someone, you build a nest and have little kakos with that someone. Such is the script. If you like each other you stay together, and if you don't, you move away and find another love. Many elect to stay on and many choose to go separate ways and find new loves. No one keeps count.

Even though Lucille was a hotly pursued kako catch, it was Rodney who first fell in love and left the Jacaranda Condominium to move in with his partner from another condominium a little distance away. He met Sarah Crow quite by chance while he was loafing, with nothing to do and nowhere to go. He'd been flying aimlessly (which we all often did) and came across this young female kako bathing in a roadside puddle. There are few things as attractive as a young female kako with wet feathers. That's where the romance started - you could call it a poolside romance - and soon they were inseparable.

Maybe there too he used well-practised openers like, 'What's your name?' and 'Let me get you some breakfast!' They had proved effective in the past in paving the way to longer conversations.

"She's something special, Kaki," Rodney was so full of awe he could hardly mention her name. "She's all I ever wanted as a partner: good looking and wise, knows when to open her mouth and when to keep it closed."

It didn't take them long to start looking for their own nest. When Rodney came along and told us he was leaving the Jacaranda Condominium to make a new home, Lucille looked at me desperately, as if I could do something to stop him. I looked away, knowing I could not, should not.

Mama Alice was her familiar self and gave my brother her usual advice before he left. There's always sorrow when losing one from the fold, but we knew not to dwell on it. When things change, you just begin again.

I think I felt it more than the others. We'd grown up together, Rodney, Lucille and I, but we were 'the boys'.

From the time Mama Alice hatched us from her eggs, we had done everything together.

He was more a friend than family to me and even though I tried not to show it, I was sad. But I wished him well and gave him a peck on his neck before he flew off to live with his bride in their condominium.

Parting from people we love will always be sad, but the sun rises every day the same way. It dies in the evening, and night cloaks the day. Life goes on, as it has always done. Accepting the need to make changes is part of learning to live.

Sadder things happened in the Jacaranda Condominium than Rodney going away.

It was early morning on a gloomy day, and there was a big commotion with everyone shouting at the tops of their voices.

"It's Roy, it's Roy," kako voices rang out.

We all flew down to see what was wrong. Old Roy was lying on the ground with his beak open. He was gasping for breath, his chest heaving in painful movements. His eyes were glazed too, as if he was looking at the "faraway" sky through the sprawling branches of the jacaranda tree.

We all gathered around him and it wasn't difficult for us to figure out that Old Roy was breathing his last. Everyone watched silently as he fluttered his wings in one last attempt and closed his eyes.

That was the end of the old warrior; the silver lining kako who had seen it all, the one who had flown with the geese to see the world, had taken his last look at life and said a silent good-bye.

"I saw him lean out and fly, his one good wing flapping away and even the broken one was moving," Dincy Crow described to us all, having seen Roy's last struggle.

"I think he must have wanted to die flying," Mama Alice concluded.

That was the end of Roy Crow who had taught us all to fly. We all sang his praises at the wake and many kakos from the vicinity came by to see old Roy lying dead and pay their last respects.

The one who mourned most was Granny Vini, who silently watched it all, perched on her high jacaranda branch. She had been Old Roy's companion and friend and had shared pleasant days and times worth a lifetime with Roy, the crow who knew how best to fly.

She mourned without words and sound, for there was nothing for her to shout about and what had to be said had been said. The memories of silver linings and such – would do for the rest of her days.

Rami Crow laid one egg and everyone came to see the nest where the single white egg was given pride of place. It shone like a little moon on the twig floor of their kako nest. Mooshu Crow made it a point to explain (to whoever listened) about this new method of 'birth control,' and how it was better to raise one small kako and give him all your love than to have it spread among many.

"We always thought it would be better this way," said the proud 'one egg' parents.

That is how Marlon Crow came to this world, no brothers, no sisters, just Marlon, and before he could open his eyes he started bawling very loudly to announce his arrival. Little as he was, he had a big mouth and a piercing scream, which he used liberally, shattering the peace of the entire Jacaranda Condominium. Rami Crow was in seventh heaven and Mooshu was fast climbing beyond cloud nine. They were the prototype - dancer Rami and loafer Mooshu – for the new kako concept of reducing numbers in a nest, and successfully launching a new way of life in the kako world called 'family planning.'

One thing remained to be seen, of course: whether this little fellow would come to be known among the jacaranda crowd as 'One Egg Marlon.'

'Right turn Eddie' who had become a member of the Elder's Club, had taken a new leaf in life to train young kakos to win shit-shooting championships. He had become a full-time trainer and a competition umpire.

"I want to try and get my teams to compete internationally if possible, maybe invite kakos from all over the world to come here and have a great time shitting on the Great Ones." That was his plan. "No point in pitting ourselves against those silly cathedral pigeons, we can always beat them hollow!"

Eddie was looking for stiffer opposition. He'd also started a new thing to go looking for people who pretended to be statues on busy streets, and give them a taste of a bit of kako wacko. Eddie always took some of his pupils along to share this amusement, and give them some practice too. It must have been a lot of fun, there were a fair number of Great Ones who painted themselves in shimmering green or bronze, and stood motionless on pedestals, pretending to be statues to entertain kids. Sometimes they were soldiers, sometimes wild men, and sometimes angels with trumpets, all standing absolutely still. Well, that was fine, and little children stood around in awe with open mouths. That was when Eddie and his troop busted the whole act, the show gone to smithereens and the kids laughed even more at the soldier or angel who'd got a full blast of crow shit on his head.

That was 'Right Turn' Eddie's latest line of entertainment, and when I had last met him he was busy making plans for the international competition of shit-shooting he hoped to stage one day.

Black Berry Crow faced a grave problem requiring a complete change to his entire lifestyle. Great Ones had dug drains and flattened the land surrounding his condominium. Big machines with oversized wheels levelled the surface and cut down all the bushes and trees, chopping them into little pieces they could take away to burn.

The Great Ones were building something big and blocky.

And, so came the end to Blackberry Crow's fruit-laden blackberry bush. Uprooted and removed, it awaited disposal, its branches still laden with the deep blue-black fruit our Blackberry loved so much.

He was no fool; Blackberry had scouted around for other blackberry bushes every time he flew out of his home ground, just in case he needed to find alternatives. Unfortunately, Blackberry's efforts had been in vain, as he never found another blackberry bush even remotely close to his home. No blackberries, no food for our Blackberry Crow.

We all thought he would go away, as far as he had to go to find a place where he could eat his precious blackberries again. This was a logical conclusion, as no one had ever seen him feeding on anything else.

Some kakos even went to meet him to say good-bye.

But he stayed on! I guess home, friends and family were more important to Blackberry Crow than his berries.

In the days that followed, we watched his buoyant personality sink lower and lower, as he attempted life without his berries. Everyone knew he was struggling. Some kakos even laughed or made faces at him when they saw him picking up scraps of vegetable at the market and eating them. But, he persevered.

It wasn't long before he conquered himself.

"Life has to go on, Kaki." That's what he told me. "Things change, things always change. When I had berries I ate them, now I have no berries, so I eat anything."

When he said that, I remembered how our thinking kako, Cameron Crow with the head tilt, used to say that it was all in the mind.

Though we did not have the thought-life of Cameron Crow or the words to frame such ideas, we knew life is in the clouds and in the sunshine, brimming with berries or bulldozed flat, and our experience of it was a simple matter of how we chose to look at it.

Blackberry Crow chose his way, managing his mind and learning to survive without his bountiful berries. But the name stuck on and no one called him anything but Blackberry Crow.

After Stanley's death, Alice lived alone for a long time. She was the perfect mother to us; and as time took its toll, she too settled into an ordinary kako life of waking to face a day, eating to survive, and waiting for the sun to set to go to sleep and end the day. No shame in that, it's what most kakos did in their senior years.

Alice met Dickson Crow and Deidre Crow at the market place. They had a lot in common: same age, same lot in life, their children grown and flown. On a typical day, the couple would wonder about in close proximity to their home to make the hours in the day pass lightly and quickly. But that day they had flown a greater distance than usual, and stopped at the market place for a bite to eat. Here they flew into Alice.

"They are very nice, Kaki, lovely to sit and talk to, and they are so very friendly."

That's what Mama Alice told me when she returned home late in the evening.

It seemed that Dickson and Deidre lived in a condominium rented mostly by elderly kakos. They had invited Alice to visit them and meet their friends, maybe stay a few days, see where they lived and what they did.

Alice flew off one morning, at the invitation of her new-found friends. Something told me that she wasn't just visiting, it could be more than just meeting the 'D' kakos, as she used to refer to them.

She returned to the Jacaranda a few days later, but she didn't come alone. She flew in with a new-found friend, Albert: that's what she told us, but it was clear to see there was more than just friendship between Albert and Alice (or should I say the two 'A' kakos)!'

She said a fond good-bye to her friends at the jacaranda tree and then to her family. Granny Vini, Lucille and me. I always thought I was very special to her, and I think I was right. She hugged and kissed me, and muttered the things mothers say to children in whispers, where meaning is more than what is said and words cease to matter. I responded with equal affection and I felt a tide swelling inside which I did my best to hide.

She'd found a new life with a new kako and was moving out to share with Albert Crow what was left of her days.

We all watched them go, and I kept looking at the sunset-filled sky till Mama Alice was just a speck on the horizon and ultimately vanished from our sight. I was happy for her, but sad for myself. I knew I would miss her, but to be honest, I have to admit I have missed her more than I thought I would. She was irreplaceable, as a mother and as a friend.

15

There Never was a 'Forever'

I've been wondering for some time what I should say to my readers when I come to the end of this book. About my life as a kako, I mean: personalities I have known, where I lived, and what happened in our kako world. It isn't easy to record everything as I am writing solely from memory, having kept no notes or diaries. It's possible I may have missed some events or occurrences here and there. I confess I may have ignored some things purposely too: we certainly were no angels with halos and harps all our lives. We had our share of shadowy shades, not often, but enough to remind ourselves they should be kept in the closet. I wouldn't want the one book I have written to slander my own kind.

I've done my best, and told you my story: our story. It's very different to the way the Great Ones think of us: 'Stupid crows,' as they like to define our entire clan, or, when they want to be more insulting, 'Those ugly black birds.' Perhaps, after reading my story, you might reconsider who is ugly and who is stupid. Even a Great One may never look at a crow in quite the same way again. If that is true, I am glad I have put all this down, so there is a kako's version of life on this planet available to everyone, to explain who we really are for anyone who is interested in hearing our side of the story.

I could write a lot more, but then I might bore you with trivialities that do not mean much. I didn't write this book to fill pages, but to give you the gist of what my life has been from the time I was born. There were Alice, Stanley, Rodney and Lucille to begin with. Then came the others: Granny Vini, Roy Crow, Mooshu, Rami, Lizzybird, Victor Crow and a host of other characters I have already told you about. It was important to include my friends Croco Martin and Tony Monkey too, whose stories are sad but necessary to your future view of the world we share. I met some wonderful kakos and did many delightful things. That's what has filled all these pages - totally original, real-life stuff that I, the one and only Kakiyan, experienced.

Those days have become these days and the count has become longer and longer, and as the Great Ones say, the years have rolled by and the world has become older. I am still here, strutting around the Jacaranda Condominium doing the things I always did. A little after Alice left the nest, Lucille too found her knight in 'not so shining' armour. One good thing for us all is that she didn't have to leave the jacaranda tree to make a new home. 'More-to-life Cameron' decided to add my sister to his life. He must have done his famous 'Cameron Tilt' and proposed to her. Lucille, though pretty, had always been (in my opinion) a bit too choosy. She looked for a partner from the top shelf and ended up almost choice-less as the years took their toll (as they sometimes do). She must have been relieved when Cammy Crow proposed. He isn't anything much to boast about, but at least he can think.

Granny Vini was the happiest of us all. She saw Lucille settled before she closed her eyes. After Mama Alice went away to become Mrs Albert, Vini had taken it upon herself to ensure Lucille found someone suitable from the same neighbourhood.

As for me, I never fell in love. Oh, no! It wasn't that I didn't want to, but somehow it never happened the way other kakos talked about it. A little excitement was often there with kako females, if you know what I mean, that extra beat of the heart which falls like a thunder clap. But it always died down before a heart storm started, kind of like a passing shower or moonlight interrupted by high-sailing dark clouds. Shine and gone or rain and gone, either way soon enough, it was gone.

And so I got old; same old Kakiyan and same old Jacaranda Condominium, living the same old days that came and went, constant as day and night. A piece of papaw here, a steal of cheese there, loafing by the beach and waiting for the boats to come in, or flying along the river to Croco Martin's sandbank, just for the heck of it.

Such was my life, and I loved it.

I've always watched the geese fly overhead and wondered whether I'll be there to see them come back when the seasons change. That's what happens when you get old; you really can't plan too far ahead as you don't know when it will be time for you to go. 'Travel light' is the answer to that question, as old Roy Crow once said to me in his uncanny wisdom:

"There's not much one can do, boy, when the wings aren't as strong as they used to be and the heart begins to slow down. It's only the spirit that remains, and that too gets dented with age."

I've had a great life, as good as any that I've known and better than most. There are so many things to be grateful for. I look back and thank the Good Lord for blessing me so much. If it came to a matter of counting, the tally has always been the good side winning by a wide margin.

Sometimes I've felt like going away, maybe step onto a train and go far and far till it all ends. Or do what Victor

Crow did: sail the seas in a ship that never returns, go to different places I've only heard of, and maybe die there. But those are just idle thoughts like all the rest we ponder when we have nothing else to do. Free minds and free thoughts, just cheese castles we build inside of our heads. I am not the adventurous type to vanish on a train, or cruise away on a ship; maybe when I was younger it might have been different and possible, but now I am old, and I know I am not what I used to be.

Things have changed, they always do.

EPILOGUE

And when the winds began to blow from the north this year, the geese flew in as usual. The reed-covered river bank was once again a home for all kinds of birds, who came to nest as they had always done, and to lay their eggs.

The sun started moving south, the days grew shorter, and the nights became longer and colder. The geese cackled loudly as usual, to announce their arrival. Everything repeated itself, just as they always did: the weather, the birds, the shorter days and the long cold nights. Nothing ever changes in the greater plan; life revolves around an invisible circle, ordered to do so and obedient to that command.

Except that this time there was no Kakiyan watching, from his perch in the Jacaranda Condominium.

He was gone. Somewhere between the time the geese flew away, and the time they came back, Kakiyan said his farewell to the world. Does it really matter how he went, or who came to say good-bye to him at his kako wake? He'd enjoyed his life, flown where he wanted, and lived life to the fullest as best as he could.

The places in which he did these things don't have anything by which to remember him, except for a few snippets of recollections, that might linger in some fellow-kako minds.

That he was:

Kakiyan Crow,
Son of Stanley Crow and Alice Crow,
brother to Rodney Crow and Lucille Crow,
brother-in-law of Sarah Crow and Cameron Crow.

That is all there is to it.
Of course, then, there is the book that he wrote,

KAKIYAN, THE STORY OF A CROW

Printed in Great
Britain
by Amazon